T0286985

THE WOMAN WHO LOWERED THE BOOM

ALSO BY DAVID HANDLER

THE STEWART HOAG MYSTERIES

The Man Who Died Laughing
The Man Who Lived by Night
The Man Who Would Be F. Scott Fit gerald
The Woman Who Fell from Grace
The Boy Who Never Grew Up
The Man Who Cancelled Himself
The Girl Who Ran Off with Daddy
The Man Who Loved Women to Death
The Girl With Kaleidoscope Eyes
The Man Who Couldn't Miss
The Man in the White Linen Suit
The Man Who Wasn't All There
The Lady in the Silver Cloud
The Girl Who Took What She Wanted

THE BERGER AND MITRY MYSTERIES

The Cold Blue Blood
The Hot Pink Farmhouse
The Bright Silver Star
The Burnt Orange Sunrise
The Sweet Golden Parachute
The Sour Cherry Surprise
The Shimmering Blond Sister
The Blood Red Indian Summer
The Snow White Christmas Cookie
The Coal Black Asphalt Tomb
The Lavender Lane Lothario

THE BENJI GOLDEN MYSTERIES

Runaway Man
Phantom Angel

FEATURING HUNT LIEBLING

Click to Play

FEATURING DANNY LEVINE

Kiddo
Boss

THE WOMAN WHO LOWERED THE BOOM

A STEWART HOAG MYSTERY

DAVID HANDLER

THE MYSTERIOUS PRESS
NEW YORK

For the Big O, with immense gratitude

◆

THE WOMAN WHO LOWERED THE BOOM

Mysterious Press
An Imprint of Penzler Publishers
58 Warren Street
New York, N.Y. 10007

First Mysterious Press edition

Interior design by Maria Fernandez

Library of Congress Control Number: 2023918644

Cloth ISBN: 978-1-61316-513-3
eBook ISBN: 978-1-61316-514-0

10 9 8 7 6 5 4 3 2 1

Printed in the United States of America
Distributed by W. W. Norton & Company

CHAPTER ONE

"It's Norma," said the voice on the other end of the phone. "Please tell me I didn't wake you. I know it's *kind of* early."

Lulu, my faithful, breath-challenged basset hound, certainly thought so. She grumbled unhappily at me from her leather armchair before circling around three times and falling back into a grumpy doze.

I glanced at Grandfather's Benrus on my wrist. "It's not *kind of* early, Norma. It's five twenty-seven A.M. But, no, you didn't wake me."

Hell, no. I'd been sitting at the Stickley library table that served as my desk for nearly two hours, wearing my Sex

Pistols T-shirt under a ragged old turtleneck sweater, torn jeans, and Chippewa boots while I listened to the Ramones on vinyl, drank espresso, and stared out the window at our sixteenth-floor view of predawn Central Park with my stomach in knots, waiting, waiting for her to call. An author is a performer who works alone on paper, and I was still in character. Still writing the book, still living the book, still *inside* of the book.

Until Norma said otherwise.

Merilee had spared no expense to furnish the office for me when she decided it was time for me to move back into the prewar doorman building on Central Park West, which I'd called home back when we were New York City's "it" couple. She was Merilee Nash, Joe Papp's most beautiful and gifted rising star. I was Stewart Hoag, the tall, dashing young author of *Our Family Enterprise,* the best-selling novel that had prompted the *New York Times Book Review* to hail me as "the first major new literary voice of the 1980s." I was a shining star—right up until I got writer's block, snorted my career and marriage up my nose, and got booted back to my crummy unheated fifth-floor walk-up on West Ninety-Third Street, where I eked out a highly undistinguished living as a ghostwriter of celebrity memoirs.

But it was now the spring of 1995 and I'd found my voice again. Or I believed I had. I'd just devoted the past two years of my life to *My Sweet Season of Madness,* a rollicking tale about my wild postcollege years in the graffiti-strewn, crime- and rat-infested punk-music world of New York City in the seventies. When I'd shown the first 150 pages of it to the Silver Fox, Alberta Pryce, my highly respected literary agent, she pronounced them so thrilling that she sold my work in progress, sight unseen, to Norma Fives, the brilliant young editor in chief of Guilford House. Norma was still in her twenties but had such a razor-sharp literary mind that the publishing world was calling her the next Bob Gottlieb. And such was Alberta's reputation that Norma hadn't hesitated to offer me a lucrative contract even though I'd refused to show her a single page of it until it was done—or at least as done as it could be without an editor's input. Alberta had read the finished manuscript two days ago and was wildly enthusiastic. Trust me when I tell you that Alberta is seldom wildly enthusiastic. With my blessing, she'd phoned Norma, calmly told her "Hoagy's ready for you to have a look," and messengered it over to her, all 378 pages of it.

And now I sat there, my heart pounding, waiting for her to say something. Anything. What she finally said was "So . . ."

And what I said was "So . . ."

"I've read your novel twice. The first time I approached it the way a reader would. The second time I read it as an editor and marked it up. I've just finished, but I figured despite the hour you'd be somewhat anxious to get my response."

Norma, like the Silver Fox, often worked straight through the night.

I breathed in and out impatiently. "And . . .?"

"And what, Hoagy? Oh, I forgot, we've never worked together before. I never have editorial conversations with authors over the phone. That's what's wrong with the modern publishing business. Nobody talks to anybody in person anymore. And, my God, now that we have America Online, people don't even talk on the phone. They just dash off stupid emails to each other. God, I hate those things. I'll be waiting at the entrance to Central Park, across the street from your building at six o'clock, which is to say in thirty minutes. It should be getting light out by then."

"I'll be there, Norma. But, seriously, you're really not going to give me even the slightest inkling of your reaction until then? You're just going to torment me for thirty solid minutes? Make that twenty-nine."

"It's payback time. Did you show me pages of the book when I begged you to?"

"You know what, Norma? You're a genuine piece of work."

"You know what, Hoagy? You're not the first person who's told me that."

I brushed my teeth and shaved in my office bathroom, then made my way down the corridor, Lulu following me just in case there might be a can of 9Lives mackerel for cats and extremely weird dogs in it for her. In addition to my office at the far end of the corridor, there were two guest bedrooms and a bath. A door that Merilee had installed for my privacy opened into the living room, which she had furnished in mission oak after I left, and not just any mission oak but signed Gustav Stickley craftsman originals, each piece spare, elegant, and flawlessly proportioned. My favorite piece, aside from the writing table she'd chosen for me, was the oak-and-leather settee set before the floor-to-ceiling windows in the living room overlooking the park. I would stretch out there every day after lunch and hand edit my morning's work before I returned to my office to retype it on my solid steel 1958 Olympia portable. The door to the master bedroom suite, which was off the entry hall, was closed, the phone unplugged from its wall outlet. Merilee—which is to say jet-lagged, thoroughly exhausted Merilee—was no doubt still fast asleep, having just returned after *finally* finishing principal photography in Budapest, London, and Pamplona on the trouble-plagued remake of *The Sun Also Rises* with Mr. Mel Gibson. The director had been fired, the director had been rehired, and on and on it went. But it was done now, aside from some looping that she could do in a New York sound studio.

I opened a can of mackerel for Lulu to devour while I fetched my 1933 Werber A-2 flight jacket from the entry hall closet and put it on. It was spring but still chilly in the early morning. Lulu joined me, licking her chops, and out the door we went. Rode the elevator down to the lobby, where Arturo, the building's new morning doorman, was already on duty in his brass-buttoned uniform and spotless white gloves. He wished me a polite good morning as he held the door open for us. I returned the greeting. Then we crossed Central Park West in dawn's early light, and, sure enough, there was Norma Fives waiting for me at the entrance to Central Park with her book bag thrown over her shoulder, looking uncannily like a geeky college sophomore in her thick horn-rimmed glasses. The hottest editor in publishing was five feet tall, bony nosed, and so scrawny she couldn't have weighed more than ninety-five pounds. Her blunt hairdo looked as if she'd cut it herself in the bathroom mirror with a pair of poultry shears. Throw in the boxy, shapeless knit sweater, skirt, and pair of black-and-white saddle shoes she was wearing, and Norma bore an eerie resemblance to one of those nutso, skinny-armed little girls in Roz Chast's brilliant *New Yorker* cartoons. But Norma was not to be trifled with. She was ruthless and tough as nails. There was a famous story about her in the publishing world. Back when she'd been an entry-level editorial assistant, she decided she'd taken all the high-decibel personal abuse she could tolerate from the editor in chief at the weekly editorial meeting and hurled a heavy black Stanley Bostitch stapler across the conference table at the nasty bitch, coming within an inch of blinding her. Naturally, she was fired. But she was so talented another house had hired her by the end of the day.

She bent down and patted Lulu, then gazed up at me, her face revealing nothing in the streetlamps. "I wish you'd stop being so tall."

"Possibly you're just a shrimp."

After she'd stuck her tongue out at me, we started into the park, Norma steering us in the direction of the playing fields.

"How's Very doing?" I asked her.

At twenty-eight, hyperactive hipster Romaine Very was the top homicide detective in New York City. He and I, through no fault of my own, had ended up joined at the hip on several murders. The latest was just this past fall.

When we'd paid a visit on a suspect together, Very took a bullet in the thigh that nicked his femoral artery and nearly cost him his life. Strangely, we'd grown to become friends. Even more strangely, when he'd met Norma on another case, they fell madly in love. They had a host of neuroses in common, plus they were both brilliant. Very had a degree in astrophysics from Columbia.

"He's back catching cases again," Norma answered. "Says his leg is about eighty-five percent there. It still aches at night after a long day on his feet." She gazed up at me. "You saved his life, you know."

"Did not. That was Lulu, not me."

"He doesn't remember it that way."

"Well, I do. And so does Lulu."

Lulu let out a bark to confirm it. She has a mighty big bark for someone with no legs.

We arrived at a nice open stretch of dewy lawn that we had completely to ourselves since it was still barely six o'clock. Norma plopped her book bag down, opened it, and pulled out a bright pink Frisbee.

"Go out for one," she commanded me with a wave of her tiny hand.

"*Go out for one*? Who are you, Joe Pisarcik?"

"Joe who?"

I sighed. "Sometimes I forget you're still a child."

I ran across the grass and she flung the Frisbee my way with a quick flick of her wrist. I caught it and sent it back to her. And so we played Frisbee for the next five minutes instead of talking about the novel to which, as I believe I mentioned, I'd devoted the last two years of my life. Lulu barked at me to let me know she wanted in. She likes to play Frisbee. She doesn't showboat like those slobbery golden retrievers that leap high in the air to make the catch, but she's sure-footed and catches anything that comes her way. I tossed her one and she caught it in her mouth and ambled back to me to deliver it.

"Attagirl, Lulu. Oh, hey, Norma, you don't mind mackerel-scented saliva on your Frisbee, do you?" I tossed it to her.

Norma caught it, and blurted out, "It's exhilarating, heartbreaking, and so full of hard-fought wisdom that you totally knocked me on my ass. You nailed it, you bastard. It's the best novel any American author has written in at least five years."

I stood there motionless, waiting for the other shoe to drop. "But . . . ?"

"There's no but. We're going all in. It's going to be our big Christmas literary novel. Major promotional campaign, national author tour, the works. I know from Alberta how long and hard you've battled. Twelve years it took you to claw your way back. But you did it, Hoagy. You're back." She peered at me suspiciously in the early light. "You're not saying anything? Why aren't you saying anything?"

I swallowed, breathing in and out. "I'm just . . . stunned. I *thought* it was good. Every morning when I woke up, I was so anxious to get to the typewriter that my fingers would itch. And Alberta kept *telling* me it was good. But until you hear it from your editor . . ."

"It's not good, tall person. It's *great*. A major, major novel. Mind you, it's not perfect. I've marked it up. Made suggestions for tweaks here and there. Mostly, you got tired every once in a while and settled for an observation that could have been just a tiny bit sharper. But I'm a real stickler that way. I want every word to be perfect."

"As do I. Just let me at it. I'll work my tail off."

"The manuscript's in my bag. If you could get it back to me in a couple of weeks, that would be great. I really, really want to move on it. Get the sales force involved, the marketing weasels . . ."

"Sure. Absolutely. Anything you say."

She stowed the Frisbee in her book bag, pulled out a blanket, stretched it out on the lawn, lay down on her back, and stared up at the sky. I did the same. She took my hand and squeezed it. "Admit it, this is better than a phone call."

"Much better."

"We can feel the earth under us. And see the stars."

"I can't see any stars. It's cloudy."

"They're still there, doofus. Hoagy, can I ask you a personal question?"

"Norma, you can ask me anything."

"Did you really do all those things? Take all that LSD? Ride around to after-hours dance clubs in Spanish Harlem at four in the morning on your Norton motorcycle with Reggie Aintree?"

"I never say in the book that it was Reggie."

"Okay, so you call her Angie. But everyone knows you two were a hot item."

Indeed, Reggie Aintree was the first great love of my life. A gifted poet. Daughter of Eleanor Aintree, the Pulitzer-winning poet, and Richard Aintree, the enigmatic author of the classic novel *Not Far from Here.*

"Did those things really happen?" she pressed me.

"They happened. I did crack up my bike and I was in a coma for three days."

"I think five days would be better."

"Five it is, Coach."

"Thanks. I like to feel as if I'm contributing something."

"You did a lot, Norma. You believed in me. Or at least believed what Alberta was telling you. Does she know you've read it?"

"I called her before I called you. She's delighted, of course." Abruptly, Norma sat up and said, "Okay, our editorial session is over. If you have any questions or can't make out my handwriting, call me. If there are any notes you hate, ignore them. It's *your* book."

She reached into her book bag for my manuscript, which was stuffed in a padded mailing pouch, and handed it to me. Then we stood up, she folded her blanket and put it in the book bag with her Frisbee.

I said, "Tell Very I said hey. I'm glad he's back on the job."

"And say hey to Merilee for me. I'm glad she's home."

"Her body's home but her brain is still somewhere out over the Atlantic. I'm going to wake her up and give her the good news. But before I do, I just need one last reality check. I'm not hallucinating this, am I? It's really happening."

"It's really happening. I'm about to publish the best novel of my career. And I'm *not* going to pressure you to write another one because I know that's how you got in trouble before. You don't ever have to write another book for me or anyone else as far as I'm concerned. But if you do, I get first dibs. Deal?"

"Deal. But wait a sec . . ." I took her book bag off her shoulder, gave her a hug, and kissed her on the cheek.

She gazed up at me like a wide-eyed kid. "I swear, I'll never forget this moment for as long as I live."

"Trust me, neither will I."

◆

To my astonishment, Merilee was actually up and about when Lulu and I returned, although she was moving as if Count Dracula had just put her in a trancelike state. Her facial expression was so utterly blank that I found myself searching her throat for fang marks. She was making espresso and also putting a load of her travel laundry into the bright red Swedish high-efficiency washing machine. But she was so zonked it wouldn't have surprised me if she'd tried to make the espresso in the washing machine instead.

Merilee's waist-length golden hair was tied up in a bun. She was wearing a Turnbull & Asser target-dot silk dressing gown that had been mine until she stole it from me. There aren't many downsides to living with a gorgeous six-foot-tall movie star, but one of them is that she constantly "borrows" my clothes and doesn't give them back because they look better on her than they do on me.

"Well, look at you . . ." she murmured at me, yawning hugely as she poured us out two cups of espresso, handed me mine, and took a grateful gulp of hers. "Out before dawn, all bright-eyed and pink cheeked." She smiled down at Lulu. "And how are *you,* sweetness?" Lulu stood before the refrigerator and let out a low whoop. She wanted an anchovy treat. She likes them cold because the oil clings better. Merilee opened the jar and gave her one, then petted her. "Darling, why is Lulu all wet?"

"We were playing Frisbee in Central Park."

Merilee arched an eyebrow at me. "Since when did you two start living in a Neil Simon play?"

"Actually, we had a third playmate."

"Who was the other . . . ?" Merilee was still far from alert, but thanks to the espresso, she'd finally noticed the mailer pouch under my arm. "What's that you've got there, Mister?"

"What, this old thing? Just my novel. Norma called me at five twenty-seven A.M. to tell me she'd read it twice and was ready to talk about it. It seems she doesn't like to have editorial conversations over the phone so we met in the park at dawn—although she still wouldn't give me so much as a hint of her reaction until the three of us had tossed a Frisbee around for a while. Then she finally told me . . . are you sitting down . . . ?" As a matter of fact, Merilee was sitting on the floor, taking a kitchen towel to Lulu, who was wriggling with pleasure. "Good, because I don't want you to hurt yourself when you faint. Are you ready?"

"Ready for what, darling?"

"She said that it's the best novel any American author has written in at least five years. She thinks it exhilarating and—and heart-breaking and filled with hard-fought wisdom. She wants to make it Guilford House's major Christmas release. Ad campaign, national author tour, the works. She has some editorial notes that I have to spend the next two weeks going over. But I did it, Merilee. I found my way back. I'm not a one-hit wonder. I'm not a shlock celebrity ghostwriter. I'm an *author.* Actually, she called me a major, major talent—but you know how I don't like to brag."

Merilee didn't say a word. Just sat there on the floor, tears streaming down her face. I joined her there and hugged her and she hugged me back as Lulu climbed all over us with her tail thumping. If there were three happier creatures on the planet at that particular moment, I'd like to know their names and addresses.

"Oh, darling, I'm so . . . so . . ." Merilee broke off, sobbing. "So proud of you. This feels like Christmas morning when I was a little girl, except I can't stop crying. It definitely calls for a major celebration tonight. What would you say to a blood-rare steak for two at

Peter Luger, onion rings, creamed spinach, and at least two bottles of Dom Pérignon?"

"That's a definite yes on the Dom Pérignon, but you've been gone so long that I want you all to myself tonight. I was thinking more along the lines of one of your breakfasts for dinner—just us, right here."

"Let me guess . . . buckwheat pancakes and sausages?"

"That would be a no."

"Waffles and fried chicken?"

"Ooh . . . but no."

"Scrapple?"

"That would be a hell no."

"Wait, I've got it—thick-cut bacon, farm-fresh eggs sunny-side up, and a huge mound of my home fries with sautéed peppers and onions."

"Ding-ding-ding."

Merilee studied me with her mesmerizing green eyes. "Are you sure you don't want a big night out on the town?"

"Positive. I want to gaze out our living room windows with you at the greatest city on earth and just soak it all in."

"You've got yourself a deal, handsome. But only on one condition . . ."

"Name it."

"You join me, naked, in the bedroom under the covers within thirty seconds, because I have an overwhelming desire to show you how much I appreciate you."

"And I have an overwhelming desire to let you."

Actually, it was more like ten seconds before we were naked under the covers.

Later—quite a bit later—the bedside phone rang. She'd plugged it back in when she got up. I fumbled for it and answered it.

"Hi, Hoagy. It's me again."

"Me" being Norma, who was at her office now. I could hear phones ringing and voices in the background. Her own voice sounded decidedly different than it had in the park. Ill at ease.

My mind immediately went to the worst-possible place. "Our deal's dead, isn't it? What made you change your mind?"

"I haven't changed my mind about your book, you ninny. Don't be such an author. No, this is something else. I, um, I've received a sort of death threat in this morning's mail, and I was wondering if you'd mind dropping by the office."

"I'd be happy to, but I'm not sure what kind of help I can offer. This sounds more like a job for the police."

That was when I heard the familiar voice of Romaine Very holler, "Just shut up and get your ass over here, dude, will you? And I mean *now*!"

◆

Guilford House was headquartered on the twenty-sixth and twenty-seventh floors of a soul-free upended-shoebox office building on Sixth Avenue and West Fifty-Second Street. Lulu and I caught a cab down. The day was still cloudy and cool so I'd gone with the gray flannel suit from Strickland and Sons, Savile Row, a soft navy-blue merino wool shirt, yellow knit tie, and my trench coat and fedora.

The elevator doors opened at the twenty-sixth floor on a spare-every-expense reception area. There was the Guilford House logo on the wall. There were four white plastic chairs and a matching white plastic coffee table with a handful of Guilford House catalogs on it.

A blank-faced receptionist was seated behind a desk. When I gave her my name, she called Norma's office, listened for a moment, and hung up without saying another word. To me she said, "I understand you know the way."

"We do. Lulu has an unerring sense of direction."

We went through a door next to the reception desk, made a sharp right turn, then a sharp left turn, then a second sharp left turn before I opened another door to a long, wide corridor. Its walls were lined with the framed covers of Guilford House's latest top-selling books. Several of them appeared to be bodice rippers featuring heroines with large, heaving breasts and heroes who resembled Fabio. There was no shortage of spine-tingling thrillers for readers who like spine-tingling thrillers. I don't. Real life tingles my spine plenty fine, thanks. Moving higher up the food chain, Guilford House had also just published an acclaimed novel by one of the most gifted black female novelists in America, a new collection of short stories by a Wyoming-based National Book Award winner and a mammoth biography of Winston Churchill.

And soon the cover of *my* book would be hanging here.

Editorial assistants were stationed at cubicles outside of their editors' offices. Low-ranking editors had the small, windowless offices on my left. Senior editors had the larger offices on my right, with windows that looked out over Sixth Avenue. Norma, being editor in chief, had the office at the end of the hall. Her editorial assistant's cubicle was currently unoccupied. That was because she was in the process of catching up with us as Lulu and I made our way down the hallway.

"Mr. Hoag?" she called out, slightly out of breath. "Hi, I'm Norma's assistant, Alissa Loeb."

"Hi, Alissa. Make it Hoagy. The only people who call me Mr. Hoag are dental hygienists, usually when they're lecturing me that I need to floss more regularly."

Alissa giggled girlishly. She was in her twenties, same as Norma, though a good six inches taller. Polished and attractive, with long, shiny black hair and gleaming brown eyes. She wore a cream-colored cashmere cardigan over a white silk blouse and pleated navy-blue slacks. "I was supposed to escort you to Norma's office but you beat me to it," she said as we arrived at her cubicle. "Congratulations on your novel. I'm reading it right now and loving it. Your words are so *alive*. I'm thrilled to be working with you." She flashed a big, inviting smile at me. "If you need *any* kind of assistance just holler, okay? That's what I'm here for."

"Thank you, Alissa. I'll do that." Bit of a suck-up, our Alissa. Not to mention a flirt. I wondered what else she was. "Would you please let Norma know I'm here?"

She flashed me another smile. "You're supposed to just barge right in."

And so I barged right in. Norma's office wasn't large or showy. Publishing execs don't invest an immense amount of ego energy on their office décor the way Hollywood execs do. Mostly, Norma's motif was clutter. There were white metal bookcases bursting with manuscripts, paperbacks, and hardcovers. Her white metal desk was piled with manuscripts. So was the carpeted floor. Even the two chairs set in front of her desk were both heaped with manuscripts. Norma was wearing the same outfit she'd had on when we played Frisbee earlier. She'd no doubt come straight here from the park. But her manner was not at all the same. She seemed highly tense.

So did Detective Lieutenant Romaine Very. Mind you, Very's normal resting state was highly tense. He suffered from a serious energy problem, as in he had too much of it. The man was so hyper that he often nodded his head rhythmically, as if he heard his own rock 'n' roll beat. His jaw was working, working on a piece of bubble gum as he stood there next to Norma's desk. Very was on the short side, five foot six, but extremely muscular, with a head of thick black hair and the sort of soulful brown eyes that make women weak in the knees. He wore a four-day growth of beard, a black crew-neck sweater, black jeans with a pager on his belt, a pair of Air Jordans, and a black hooded rain jacket. He carried his SIG Sauer P226 semi-automatic in a shoulder holster. Technically, Very worked out of the Twenty-Fourth Precinct on West One Hundredth Street. But, real world, he was the city's top celebrity homicide detective. Whenever it was someone famous, Very got the call. He had an amazingly keen mind. It also didn't hurt that his rabbi at One Police Plaza was Inspector Dante Feldman, the man who'd caught Son of Sam.

Lulu immediately let out a low whoop and scooted over to him, her tail thumping.

Very bent down and patted her affectionately, then stood back up and gave me a soul brother handshake. "Good to see you, dude."

"Likewise, Lieutenant. I understand from Norma that your leg's just about back to normal."

He grimaced slightly. "I still can't ride as many miles on my bicycle as I want, but I'm getting there. The doctor told me that I just need to be patient."

"Which is not something my Romeo happens to be good at," Norma said.

"Yo, I understand from Baby Girl that your new novel is brilliant. I've never heard her talk so glowingly about a book. Major congrats."

"Thanks. I'm absolutely thrilled. But what have I told you two about using your pet names in public?"

"It's just the three of us in here." On Lulu's low moan of protest, he quickly added, "Four of us. Besides, what's the big deal?"

"It's icky. Makes people uncomfortable." Neither of them had ever been in love before, and they still required tutoring. "So why am I here? What's up?"

Very's face tightened. "What's up is that Norma got a super old-school death threat in the mail this morning." He donned a latex glove and reached for a piece of typing paper on her cluttered desk as Norma sat there trying, and failing, to look calm. He set it on the desk before me. "Look, don't touch. We might find some prints on it."

I looked, didn't touch. It was super old-school, all right, a circa-1950s variety of death threat composed of words and letters that had been cut out of a magazine and pasted to a sheet of typing paper. It read:

Say **GOODBYE**.
You *are* a **DEAD** Woman.
This *is* no **JOKE**.

"Please tell me these weren't cut out of an old issue of *Look* magazine, because that would be too weird."

"Last Sunday's *New York Times Magazine*," Very said grimly. "And it's still plenty weird."

I nodded. "Very."

"Yeah, dude?"

"It's very weird."

"You got that right."

As I bent over to study it more closely, I discovered it gave off an old-school scent, too. "Man, this thing is out of a time warp. He even used *mucilage*. I haven't smelled that since I was in high school. It came in a glass bottle with a red rubber tip that you'd rub against the paper. I didn't know they even made it anymore."

"That's why I love this guy," Very said to Norma. "Want to know how often I hear the word *mucilage* on the job? Try never."

"I think you're making a big deal out of nothing," Norma said with gallant determination. "I reject manuscripts all of the time. Get angry phone calls and hate mail from authors who call me awful names. People get emotional in this business. It's nothing."

"If it's nothing," Very said, "then why did you call me to come over here ASAP?"

She lowered her gaze, swallowing. "I guess it was the way he went to so much trouble cutting up those little pieces of paper. It gives me the creeps."

"I don't blame you," I said, studying the plain white envelope it had arrived in, which had no return address on it. It was postmarked yesterday from a 10017 zip code.

"That happens to be the zip code for Grand Central Terminal," Norma said to me.

"What, you looked it up?"

"She didn't have to," Very said. "She's a postal freak. Go ahead, show him what you've got."

"Okay. Hoagy, your apartment on Central Park West in the West Seventies is one-zero-zero-two-four, yet your place on West Ninety-Third between West End and Riverside is one-zero-zero-two-*five*. Our place down on Bank Street is—"

"Okay, okay, you made your point. But I still have a question."

"Fire away," Very said, jaw working on his bubble gum.

"What are my short-legged partner and I doing here?"

Norma said, "My sweetie thinks you know a lot about the underbelly of the publishing business."

"Too much," I acknowledged.

"He wanted to get your take on it. Although if you ask me, I think he just misses you."

"Is that a fact? You should have picked up the phone, Lieutenant. We could have met for a falafel."

He let out an impatient sigh. "Can we move on, please? For starters, Norma, I want to know who you've pissed off lately. Who has it in for you. Who outright hates you."

"You mean aside from my sister?" Norma said lightly. "Okay, sure. A few semi-ugly things have happened in the past couple of weeks."

I cleared the manuscripts from one of the chairs, set them on the floor, and sat down. "Do tell."

"Well, there's Boyd Samuels."

I winced inwardly.

Very frowned. "Why does that name sound so familiar?"

"The Cam Noyes case four years ago," I said. "He was that coked-out gonzo literary agent slash scam artist who set the whole mess in motion. Four people lost their lives before it was over, but he managed to skate by serving time in a drug-and-alcohol rehab center. He resurfaced as a clean, sober, and hungry Harmon Wright Agency shithead. I tussled with him out in LA again a while back. His official title now is vice president of Literary Synergy."

"Make that *was*," Norma said, coloring slightly. "Last week, Boyd and I finalized a deal for a major seven-figure multi-book contract for HWA's biggest romance superstar. We're talking about someone who's a guaranteed number one on the *Times* best-seller list. It was a done deal—until he called me back at the end of the day to say he'd just signed a more lucrative one with another house. Didn't so much as give me an opportunity to match it or top it."

"So he just used you to inflate the asking price?"

"Precisely," she responded, her mouth tightening angrily. "I'm not someone who tolerates getting played by the likes of Boyd Samuels. I immediately called the head of the HWA literary department, your very own agent, Alberta Pryce, and lambasted him as a lying, amoral snake. I informed her that Guilford House would no longer take on any new HWA clients until and unless he was fired. Alberta, who harbors no love for Boyd herself, patiently listened to his version of the story and spoke to my rival editor. Then, after consulting with Harmon, she told Boyd to clean out his desk and get gone."

"Wait, when was this again?"

"Last week."

"So that means if Alberta *hadn't* fired him, you wouldn't have accepted my book for publication."

"What does that have to do with this?" Very asked.

"Sorry, Lieutenant. Authors have a tendency to be a tad self-centered." To Norma I said, "How did Boyd take it?"

"He totally flipped out. Showed up here unannounced and demanded to see me. The receptionist said he was highly agitated and kept hollering obscenities at her. She thought he was a crazy person."

"She's a keen judge of character. You might want to promote her. Did you see him?"

"Not a chance. I had no interest in getting into a shouting match with that lying bastard. When he refused to leave the reception area, we called building security. They escorted him out of the building, deposited him on the sidewalk, and told him to stay out or they'd have to call the police."

"And did they?"

"No, he left quietly, although an hour later he phoned me and ranted that I was an evil bitch. Called me all sorts of other names, too. When he got to *twat,* I hung up on him."

Very stood there nodding his head to his rock 'n' roll beat. "Sounds to me like we need to pay a house call on this asshole."

"By *we* do you mean you want me along?"

"I do. You know the guy better than I do."

"Sad but true. I'm supposed to be hard at work on Norma's edits right now, Lieutenant. There's considerable time pressure. But since this concerns Norma, I'm all yours. When were you thinking of . . ."

"Is now too soon?"

CHAPTER TWO

Back in his stoned-out heyday, when he was kicking the starchy literary establishment on its ass, Boyd Samuels had lived in a raw half-finished loft in Tribeca. But that was before he'd gone through rehab, donned a standard-issue HWA black Armani suit, and joined that starchy establishment. These days he lived on the tenth floor of a highly conventional—one might even say boring—postwar high-rise on Third Avenue and East Seventy-Sixth, complete with a terrace and doorman.

When the doorman announced us, Boyd told him to let us up. We found his door ajar and went in to discover that the apartment had the cheerful ambiance of a room at a Motel 6. The mismatched furniture looked as if Boyd had absconded with it from his parents' basement, although I have to confess it was hard to think of Boyd as someone who had parents. His dining table served as a workstation. Parked on it were his briefcase, a stack of manuscripts, and one of those Macintosh personal computers that are the color of cat puke. The computer was attached not only to a printer but also to a modem that was plugged into a phone jack so that he could send and receive incredibly important emails. Not that you asked me, but I'll never, ever own any of those things. I'll continue to use my 1958 Olympia solid-steel portable and Waterman fountain pen until they have to pry them from my cold, dead hands.

Boyd was seated out on his terrace in a flannel bathrobe at 11:30 A.M., unshaven, hair uncombed, guzzling Wild Turkey from the bottle and doing lines of coke. On the glass table before him were a baggie of white powder, pocket mirror, razor blade, and rolled-up five-dollar bill.

"How's it going, Boyd?" I asked, knowing perfectly well that for a recovering addict the presence of that bag of coke meant he was in serious trouble, as in circling the drain with the Ty-D-Bol Man.

He wiped his nose with the back of his hand, sniffling. "Not so great, amigo."

"So I gather. Just for starters, your memory's totally shot. I'm not your amigo, remember?"

"Can I offer you some Colombian marching powder?"

"No, thanks."

"Still got your pooch, I see."

Which prompted Lulu to bare her teeth at him menacingly.

"Not real friendly, is she?"

"No, she is. She just doesn't like you."

"Lot of that going around these days," he lamented, snorting another line.

"You remember Detective Lieutenant Romaine Very of the NYPD, don't you?"

Boyd's eyes widened in horror. "Shit, are you going to bust me for possession?"

"Not interested," Very grunted at him. "If you want to destroy yourself, go right ahead."

Boyd peered at him with a vague sense of recognition. "You look familiar. Didn't you have something to do with the Cam Noyes case?"

"A lot to do with it," Very shot back.

"Thought so." Boyd reached for the bottle of Wild Turkey. "Care for a drink, Lieutenant?"

"Little early in the day for me."

"How about you, amigo?"

"Ditto. And I'm still not your amigo."

Boyd sat back in his chair, fished a soggy tissue from the pocket of his bathrobe, and blew his nose on it loudly. "So what can I do for you guys?"

"Heard some news about you on the rumor mill," I said.

"You mean that my career as a New York literary agent is over? That I'm toast, as in see you, so long, sayonara?"

"Words to that general effect."

"All true, thanks to that little bitch Norma Fives."

"I also hear you showed up at her office and went berserk. Had to be escorted from the building by security."

"Can you blame me? The bony twat got me fired."

"Before you continue in this vein, I should warn you that Lieutenant Very happens to live with Norma."

"For real? You actually get naked with her? Can't say much for your taste in women, bro. Must be like having sex with a tuning fork."

"Why don't you shut up before I punch you in the face?"

"You do that and my lawyer will be all over you for police brutality," Boyd warned.

"Fine, then *I'll* punch you in the face," I said to him.

"Okay, okay. *Sorry*. Everybody's so damned sensitive these days. The world's gone soft. Here's the deal, straight up. I was doing my job, which is to get the most money I can for my client. When I outmaneuvered Norma, which is not easy to do, instead of showing me some respect and saying 'Good job, I'll get you next time,' the bitch got me fired. She refused to admit she'd lost. Insisted it had to be somebody else's fault. And that somebody else had to pay the price for it."

"Did you threaten her?" Very demanded.

Boyd tossed back a slug of Wild Turkey from the bottle. "I said some nasty shit to her on the phone. I would have said it to her face, except she was too cowardly to see me in person. I was pissed off. Wouldn't you be?"

"One more time. Did . . . you . . . threaten . . . her?"

Boyd conked himself on the side of his head. "I'm getting totally lost here. Where are you going with this?"

"Did you send her a death threat?"

He looked at Very blankly. "A death threat . . . ? Are you kidding me?"

"Do I look like I'm kidding you?"

"No, you look like you want to go Hannibal Lecter on my face. Read my lips, okay? I barely stayed out of jail four years ago. Do you honestly think I'd be stupid enough to send her a death threat? I'd be put away." He bent over and snorted another line of coke from the pocket mirror. "When I spoke to her on the phone, I was just trying to talk her out of calling Alberta and accusing me of unethical behavior—because I knew exactly what would happen. I didn't threaten her. If anything, I groveled. But she wouldn't listen. She's one of those people who have *principles*. And now she's destroyed my career. It's over. I don't know what I'm going to do. I don't. I just don't."

"Care for some advice?" I asked.

"Sure," he said half-heartedly. "Why not?"

"Shave, get dressed, and get straight. Then make a list of options."

Boyd let out a mocking laugh. "*What* options?"

"For starters, you'd make a good publicist at one of the publishing houses. It's a step down, but you'd work your way back up in no time."

Boyd let out another mocking laugh. "Book publicists are strictly Vassar girls who stay on the job six months before they get married to some hedge fund dick named Trevor. Hell, that's barely one rung up the ladder from the mail room."

"Which is another viable option. Some of the biggest names in show business on both coasts got their starts in the mail room."

Boyd sat there looking glum. Actually, worse than glum. Frightened. "For the past three days," he confessed, "I've been trying to climb out of a black hole and I just feel like I'm sinking in deeper."

"I've been there," I said, not unkindly. "Do you have a friend who you can call to be here with you?"

"My friends are either dead or won't return my calls," he answered bitterly.

"Then you should call the drug counselor who helped you dig your way out before. Have you got a phone number? I'll place the call for you right now."

He studied me suspiciously. "Why are you being so nice to me? You hate me."

"I don't hate you. Well, I do. But I have a duty to help you. We both fought our way out of that black hole. I don't want you to disappear into it again. I want you to get through this."

Boyd sighed miserably. "I'm down to my last two hundred bucks. I can't pay next month's rent. I don't know what I'm going to do."

"I know exactly what *I'm* going to do," Very said to him. "I'm going to leave you to wallow in your self-pity." To me he said, "Sorry, but I can't stand another second of this. He trashed the woman I love."

"Hey, I'm sorry about that," Boyd said to him. "I didn't know."

Very didn't respond. He was already heading for the door. So was Lulu.

I stayed put for a moment longer. The man was a total sleaze, yet I still felt sorry for him. "Think about what I said. Get some help, okay?"

Boyd didn't respond, just sat there defeatedly.

"You can get through this, Boyd," I said as I started for the door myself.

Boyd still didn't respond. When I turned to look at him, I realized he hadn't responded because he wasn't on the terrace anymore. Just his slippers were.

The rest of Boyd Samuels was on the sidewalk ten floors below.

◆

Very phoned it in from the kitchen, which had a sink full of dirty dishes and a trash bin stuffed with pizza boxes and junk food wrappers. It was crawling with cockroaches, but that was one of the problems that Boyd wouldn't have to worry about anymore.

Lulu and I moseyed into his bedroom, which was also a mess. The bed was unmade and not particularly fresh smelling. On an armchair in the corner there was a heap of dirty socks, boxer shorts, and an array of other wardrobe items that I didn't particularly want to look at or smell. When I opened his closet door, I found five identical black Armani suits hanging in his closet in a remarkably creepy fashion. On the floor directly underneath the five identical black suits there were five identical pairs of shined black dress shoes in a neat row. For some reason I found that even creepier. In his chest of drawers, he had a stack of starched white shirts from the laundry and not much else. It was the bedroom of an empty shell of a human being. Standing there, I felt another pang of pity for Boyd, even though he'd been a conniving schmuck. But I'd known him. He'd been in my life. And now? Now he was nothing more than another dead schmuck.

Lulu, who could read my every mood, came over and nosed my hand. I patted her. "Not to worry, girl. I'm okay."

By the time we rode the elevator downstairs, a blue-and-white had arrived and the patrolmen had covered Boyd's body with a tarp. The people who'd seen it happen were telling each other all about the horror of it, waving their arms in the air the way New Yorkers have a way of doing when their emotions are aroused.

Very spoke to one of the patrolmen while the other took witness statements from the bystanders. We were there about fifteen minutes before the coroner's van pulled up. Two of his men zipped Boyd into a black body bag, gathered him up off the sidewalk, and stowed him in the van.

I stood there watching them drive away as the shopkeeper who owned the hardware store right near where Boyd had landed hosed down the bloody sidewalk. It was a grim ritual that played out several times every day of the year in all sorts of neighborhoods. Ten minutes after the coroner's van had left, the patrol car would take off, the pavement would dry, the witnesses would disperse, and it would be as if it had never happened.

Just part of life in the city that never sleeps.

Very stood next to me on the sidewalk, jaw working on a fresh piece of bubble gum. "I'll have forensics search his place for that *New York Times Magazine* and a bottle of mucilage. Guarantee you they'll turn it up."

"I don't think so, Lieutenant. He swore he didn't send that death threat to Norma."

"I know he did, but he was lying scum."

"I don't disagree, but I still say he didn't send it. He was impulsive and confrontational. Showing up at her office and acting like a lunatic was his style. Quietly, methodically cutting out words and letters from a magazine, pasting them to a piece of paper, and sending it to her through the US Postal Service was not. Besides, he was so stoned he would have cut his fingers to pieces with the scissors. I didn't notice any cuts on his fingers, did you?"

"No," he allowed. "But if he wasn't totally freaked that a judge would lock him up for sending it, then why did he just do a Brodie off his terrace?"

"Okay, no offense, but now you're thinking like a cop, not a recovering coke addict. Let me help you out here.

He was sitting there in his bathrobe at eleven-thirty in the morning, nose down in a bag of coke, which is a sound, working definition of the road to nowhere. He was broke, depressed, his job prospects were nil—so he decided to take the nearest exit ramp."

Very mulled it over a moment. "Okay, you talked me into it. Agreed." Then he studied me curiously. "Dude, why is it that every time I see you, somebody is dead within an hour?"

"I was wondering about that myself. I guess it's just a special chemistry we share."

In response he stifled a yawn. "Sorry, I'm major sleep deprived. You're looking at the putz who was trying to sleep last night while Norma was reading your book in bed next to me and squealing with delight."

"I made her squeal with delight?"

"Several times. I had to beg her to read the last hundred pages at the kitchen table."

"I feel a bit awkward asking you this, since we're standing ten feet from the exact spot where the literary agent formerly known as Boyd Samuels just crash-landed, but Merilee and I are holding a small celebration tonight at the apartment. Champagne followed by my favorite breakfast for dinner. Would you two kids care to join us?"

"We wouldn't be intruding?"

"Not a chance. It would be a pleasure."

"Sounds good. Thanks. It's also not a bad idea. Norma doesn't usually drink because she thinks it dulls her edge, but if it's a celebration of your book, she'll have to down a glass of bubbly or two, which will make her super chatty."

"Your point being . . ."

"Maybe you can find out who else she's managed to piss off lately. As a rule, she's super tight-lipped with me about her authors. Never yammers about them. But maybe she'll yammer with you. After all, you're one of the team now."

"Sure, okay." I frowned at him. "There's something in your voice that makes it sounds as if you think she's going to get another death threat."

"Dude, I don't think she is. I know she is."

CHAPTER THREE

"Before you pop the cork on that champagne bottle, can we come to an agreement?" Norma asked me as I stood there with the chilled bottle of Dom Pérignon wrapped in a towel, ready to open it.

It was dusk now. She and Very were seated before the living room windows on the leather settee with Lulu sprawled across them. Merilee sat in one of the Morris chairs, smiling warmly at the young couple. They'd arrived separately. Very had been with a forensics team searching Boyd's apartment as well as his former office at the HWA for any traces of the makings of that death threat. They'd found nothing. I'd had zero expectation that they would, but Very wouldn't be the pro that he is if he hadn't made the effort.

Merilee was wearing a denim shirt with snaps, jeans, and cowboy boots. I'd changed out of my gray flannel suit back into the same Sex Pistols T-shirt, turtleneck sweater, and torn jeans I'd been wearing early that morning when Norma and I had tossed that Frisbee around in the park, although so much had happened since then, good, bad, and worse, that it was hard to believe it was still the same day.

An evening chill had settled in, so I'd made a fire in the fireplace, which cast a golden glow over the room.

Meanwhile, the chilled champagne flutes were sitting there on a tray on the coffee table, waiting to be filled, and I still hadn't popped the cork.

"Of course, we can come to an agreement," I said.

"Let's not let Boyd Samuels ruin your celebration."

"I'd like to second that," Very said. "And I'd also like to say that I do not want to hear the word *mucilage* spoken aloud. Deal?"

"Deal," I assured him, working the cork loose with a pop and filling our flutes.

We each took one and raised our glasses.

"This is *your* night, Hoagy," Norma said. "You've produced something magnificent. It took you a good long while, but sometimes that's how it works. Hell, Joseph

Heller didn't publish *Something Happened* until thirteen years after he wrote *Catch-22*. I am so proud to be your editor. And so thrilled that you invited us to join you this evening."

And with that, we drank.

"It's our pleasure to have you, Norma," Merilee said. "It wouldn't be a celebration without you."

"Absolutely," I said. "And I'm thrilled to be working with you. Mind you, I still haven't had time to look at any of your editorial notes . . ."

She waved me off. "They're nothing. Strictly small stuff."

"See what I mean?" Very said to me. "One sip of champagne and she becomes a softy. Two sips and her nose will start to turn pink. Just watch."

"Oh, stop," Norma said, swatting at him playfully.

The fire needed tending. I shifted the logs around and set one from the woodpile on top of it.

Norma gazed at Merilee's Oscar from the Woody Allen movie on the mantel. "Merilee, could I . . . Would you mind if I held it for a second?"

"You can take it home with you for all I care," Merilee said offhandedly.

"Yeah, sure."

"Actually, Ruth Gordon once said almost those same exact words to me in her apartment on Central Park

South when I was first starting out. Robert Altman was considering me for a role opposite her in a film and he wanted the two of us to meet. I noticed her Oscar from *Rosemary's Baby* on a bookshelf, and when I asked her if I could hold it, she said, 'Aw, you can take the goddamned thing home with you for all I care. I don't give a crap. Here, I'll get you a bag.' "

Side note: if you've ever wondered whether Merilee Nash can do a drop-dead imitation of Ruth Gordon, the answer is most emphatically yes.

I brought Merilee's Oscar to Norma. She hefted it, awe-struck. "I didn't realize they were so heavy." Then she handed it back to me carefully.

I returned it to the mantel and sat back down, gazing at Norma. "So why does she hate you?"

Norma peered at me in confusion. "Ruth Gordon hates me?"

"No, silly. Your sister. This morning you said she hates you."

"Oh, that. Maybe *hate* is too strong a word. But she definitely resents me."

"Why?"

"She's three years older than I am, okay? And when we were kids, I was Little Miss Perfect who did all my homework, got straight As and pats on the head from our folks. All that she got was yelled at for daydreaming her way through one class after another and never doing her homework. She was lazy. Didn't care about anything except hanging out with her friends and talking about boys. I'd always be in my room with my nose buried in a book. I got a scholarship to Bryn Mawr, and I've busted my tail to get to where I am. Which she also resents. She has no idea how hard I work."

"I can vouch for that," Very said, sipping his champagne. "Baby Girl puts in eighteen hours a day seven days a week."

"Same as you," she said, gazing at him fondly. "It was one of the first things we discovered we had in common."

"But not the only thing." He leaned over and kissed her.

"What does she do with herself now?" I asked as I refilled our glasses.

"She's a waitress at Scotty's diner on Broadway and West One Hundred and Third Street."

"Are you kidding me?" I said as Lulu immediately sat up and whimpered.

Norma frowned at her. "No, why would I be kidding you?"

"Which one is she, Sheila or Amy?"

"Amy. How did you . . ."

Now Lulu was letting out a low moan, her tail thumping.

"Scotty's makes absolutely *the* best tuna melt on the Upper West Side. Lulu loves the place. And she adores Amy. When I was living in my crummy fifth-floor walk-up on West Ninety-Third, we used to go there for lunch every day. I had no idea Amy was your sister. The two of you look nothing alike. She lives in Washington Heights, right? Has a boyfriend named Manny who drives a cab."

"I guess . . ." Norma responded with considerable discomfort in her voice. "We don't talk real often."

"Lulu and I haven't been going there ever since we relocated here to the high-rent district, but I'll have to stop by for lunch and say hi. Amy gives Lulu extra tuna and dotes on her. And she's always been nice to me."

"That's because you didn't grow up in the same house with her."

I shook my head at Norma. "The two of you still haven't been able to work out your childhood bullshit?"

"Nope. She can't stand me. Plus she hates that I'm thin."

"Compared to you, hon, Michelle Pfeiffer is pudgy," Merilee pointed out. "Where did you grow up?"

"Tarrytown. Our dad's the branch manager of a bank. Our mom's a receptionist in a doctor's office."

I hefted the champagne bottle. "This one is empty. Shall I open the second one or should we save it to have with dinner?"

"With dinner, I think," Merilee said. "Which is my cue to start the home fries. Lieutenant, how would you like to help me out?"

"Happy to." He grabbed his glass and started toward the kitchen with her.

Lulu ambled after him, ready for her own dinner. Or an anchovy treat. Or both.

It was not by chance Merilee had enlisted Very. I'd asked her to. Now that Norma was working on her second glass of bubbly—her nose definitely pink—I was hoping to extract some gossip from her. I got up and poked at the fire. "So, listen, on the off chance that you get another death threat in the mail tomorrow . . ."

"Hey, I thought we weren't going to talk about Boyd."

"We're not. I'm wondering who else might have reason to be pissed off at you."

Norma stared into the fire before she let out a sigh. "I've had to lower the boom lately, by which I mean I've ruined the lives of three of our authors. I've also made my assistant, Alissa, extremely unhappy. But I can't imagine any of them would send me a death threat."

"What's the deal with Alissa?"

"Last week she came in, closed my door, and said she's been an editorial assistant for four years, two of them working for me, and that she feels ready to be promoted to an assistant editor. Alissa has a lot going for her. She works hard. Reads heaps of manuscripts for me on the weekends. She's bright, gets along well with people . . ."

"But . . . ?"

"Her editorial instincts aren't as keen as they need to be. If there's a flaw in a manuscript, she's not sharp enough to spot it. Not yet anyhow. Maybe with a bit more experience, but I don't think so. Either people are born to be editors or they're not." Norma hesitated. "Plus, she's been boinking one of our married authors, which I don't consider professional."

"So what did you tell her?"

"That I didn't think she was ready. She was disappointed. Told me she'd have to start looking for a job elsewhere. I said I'd hate to lose her but if she was offered a job as an assistant editor at another house, I'd be fully supportive. She thanked me, and that was that. She's been perfectly pleasant since then. We live in the same neighborhood and still ride the subway home together after work, chattering away. It's not as if she's been hostile or anything."

"But you rejected her."

Norma nodded. "I did."

From the kitchen I heard Merilee and Very carrying on a conversation about whether Steven Seagal, his latest male action idol, was or was not a better actor than Tom Cruise. It was quite an animated conversation, especially because I happened to know that Merilee considered Tom Cruise the biggest, or I should say smallest, stiff on the planet. I could smell the bacon cooking now, as well as the onions and peppers starting to sauté in olive oil. "Now tell me about those authors whose lives you've ruined."

She crinkled her nose, which was growing pinker by the minute. "You really think this is important?"

"I do. What's more, so does Very."

"Well, okay. The first one's Alexander McCord, which you've no doubt been reading about in the *Times* because it's such an ugly controversy."

Alexander McCord was a Columbia University historian who'd been the best-selling author of eight scholarly as well as ultra-commercial biographies of American presidents. His research was detailed and impeccable, his prose lively. A snowy-haired, kindly looking man in his late fifties, Professor McCord was also a familiar TV talking head who popped up regularly with keen political insights on *The MacNeil/Lehrer NewsHour* on PBS. Everyone thought highly of him.

Until recently, that is. His newest book for Guilford House, an eight-hundred-page biography of Harry S. Truman, had been shelved just before it went to press because one of the professor's former PhD candidates, Scarlett Bloom, who'd become an assistant professor at Duke thanks to his glowing recommendation, had wangled a sneak peek at the galleys and presented credible evidence to Guilford House's lawyers that the professor had plagiarized whole passages of her PhD thesis. After conferring with the professor's lawyers, and with the professor himself, Guilford House's publisher had halted publication. Professor McCord's reputation as both a scholar and an author had taken a serious hit, and he hadn't been seen on the *NewsHour* since it happened.

"I didn't notice your name in any of the articles that I read," I said. "The decision sounded as if it came from up above."

"It did. But I'm editor in chief, so I felt it was up to me to give him the bad news."

"Did you give it to him in person or on the phone?"

"On the phone. It was a conference call. One of our lawyers and McCord's agent were also on the line."

"How did he take it when you told him?"

"That was the amazing thing. I've seen him *so* many times on TV, and he's like a kindly uncle, calm and comforting. And I love his books. I've read all of them. But when I told him we weren't going to publish his Truman bio, he went totally nuts. Screamed and hollered at me. I can still remember every word he said: 'Young lady, do you know how long I've been the number one presidential historian in America? Thirty-two years! Thirty . . . two . . . years! You haven't even been *alive* thirty-two years! How dare you, you little bitch?' "

"In other words, he took the news really well."

"It was truly horrible, Hoagy. The man's a nasty dick-head. And I'd had so much respect for him."

"Merilee warned me a long time ago that it's never a good idea to encounter one of your idols. But you did what you had to do, although it seems to me that the lawyers could have kept you out of it."

"I'm editor in chief," she repeated stubbornly. "It was up to me to tell him. This job isn't all just tossing a Frisbee in the park with a cool author and his basset hound."

"You're one tough cookie, Norma."

"Not really. After I hung up the phone, I went in the ladies' room and threw up."

"And who are the other two authors that you've lowered the boom on?"

She sipped her champagne, sighing regretfully. "I was told that our bottom line wasn't where it needed to be, so I had to drop two novelists who've been among our most popular for ages. But their sales have been slipping lately so they had to go. One of them was Richard Groat . . ."

"No way! I love his books."

"So do I, believe me."

Richard Groat was the clever creator of a high-society gentleman thief, whose novels were a modern-day homage to E. W. Hornung's *The Amateur Cracksman*, which was made into the classic 1930 film *Raffles* starring Ronald Colman. Groat had penned over a dozen *New York Times* best-sellers for Guilford House, one of which was made into the hit movie *Hot Locks* starring Michael Caine and Cher.

"Richard suffered a serious personal setback four years ago," Norma said. "His wife committed suicide by hanging herself from the chin-up bar in the doorway of his bedroom closet. She left a suicide note tied around her neck that read: *I warned you what would happen if you made me watch* Raffles *again*. He was completely shattered, and really, really late delivering his next book, which was subpar and sold miserably. And he has yet to deliver the second book of his two-book contract. In fact, I don't believe he's even written a single word. I had to give him the news in person because he now suffers from such acute anxiety that he can't leave his apartment. He's a fragile, pathetic soul. There's a tray on his kitchen counter that must have a half-dozen different prescription pill bottles on it. I felt so badly giving him the news. But I was following orders."

"How did he respond?"

"With total silence for an incredibly long time. I mean, like, two or three minutes. It was almost as if he'd gone into a trance. Then, in a very soft voice, he finally said, 'You'll regret this.' And asked me to leave." She took another sip of her champagne. "I feel like I'm blabbing your ear off. Am I?"

"No, not at all. Have you spoken to him since?"

"Nope. His contract is in the hands of our lawyers now."

I sat there thinking that Groat sounded like the most likely candidate so far to mail her that Mickey Spillane–era death threat. "And the third author?"

Norma heaved her chest. "This one hurt the most. Are you sitting down? Yes, you are. I had to give the axe to the Weaverton Elves."

"You *fired* Penelope Estes Poole?"

"I did," she confessed, ducking her head.

The Weaverton Elves was a series of cozy mysteries that had been a sentimental favorite among young girls and elderly ladies who drink tea and knit, going back thirty volumes over as many years. The Weaverton Elves were, well, how can I put this without snickering? They were a close-knit family of elves who solved whimsical crimes set in the whimsical village of Weaverton, Maine.

"I used to love them when I was a kid," Norma recalled wistfully. "But the readership has fallen twenty percent over the past three books. We don't know why. That's the crazy thing about this business. Nobody ever knows why. Maybe there aren't as many young girls who read books anymore, or maybe the elderly ladies who drink tea and knit now prefer to curl up with Stephen King. I delivered the news to Penelope in her agent's office. I'd never met her before. I thought she'd look like one of her little old knitting ladies. She's a widow, and she's definitely old—seventy-two—but a tall, regal horsewoman who's in fabulous shape. I mean, she's great looking. Absolutely radiates confidence and class."

"No surprise there. She's an Estes, one of *the* oldest, wealthiest families in New York City. An aristocrat. And when she and Harrison Poole tied the knot, she married into an even older and wealthier family than her own. I think only the Catholic Church owns more real estate in Manhattan than she does. So how did *she* take the news?"

"She was very calm and cool. But do you know what she said to me?"

"I truly can't imagine."

"She said, 'The Weaverton Elves would never allow someone like you to be happy and prosper.' "

"That wasn't very nice."

"I didn't think so."

Very appeared in the doorway now. "I've been ordered to herd you into the kitchen. The bacon's done, the potatoes are done, but Merilee doesn't want to crack the eggs until we're seated at the kitchen table."

"Not the dining table?"

"She said it's a kitchen table meal."

"And who's to argue with her?" I asked.

"Not me. Your job, dude, is to open the second bottle of champagne."

"This I can do."

As we got up and started toward the kitchen, Norma looked up at me inquisitively. "Do you think one of them sent me that letter?"

"It's entirely possible. Unless, that is, it was someone else."

"That was rather vague."

"I prefer to think of it as cryptic."

"Nope, it was vague."

"Are you going to start editing the way I talk now?"

"Goes with the territory, buster. Speaking of which, *when* are you going to start going through my edits?"

"I was a bit tied up today, in case you failed to notice," I said, inhaling the wondrousness of the bacon and home fries as we strolled into the kitchen. "But I'll set my alarm for six tomorrow morning and get right on it. Scout's honor."

Norma took a seat at the kitchen table next to Very, leaning over to give him a smooch on the cheek. "This is fun, Romeo. We should drink champagne more often."

"I've got no problem with that," he said, grinning at her.

Lulu wanted an anchovy, and who was I to say no? Then I pulled the second bottle of Dom Pérignon out of the refrigerator and worked the cork loose while Merilee got busy cracking the eggs into the cast-iron skillet she'd just cooked the bacon in.

I went around the table and refilled all our glasses.

Then Merilee began heaping our plates with bacon, potatoes, and eggs, setting them on the table along with a basket of crusty French bread. When she was done and all four us were seated before our feast, she raised her glass and said, "A toast to my favorite homicide detective, my favorite editor, and, above all, my favorite author." Before she could bring the glass to her lips, there were some low grumbling noises from underneath the table. "Who, I'd like to add, would be totally lost without my favorite basset hound."

After three thumps of Lulu's tail, we drank.

And then we dived in.

There was very little talking after that.

CHAPTER FOUR

As promised, I was seated at my desk at 6:00 A.M. with my edited manuscript and a mug of hot espresso, raring to go.

By 6:01 A.M. I hated Norma Fives with a white-hot passion.

I had good reason to. She had drawn a big red circle around the *first* line of the novel, a line that I'd rewritten at least six times so that it would grab readers by the lapels and force them to want to read what came next. The comment she'd scrawled in the margin was: *Do we really need this?*

Smart, the way she used the word *we* instead of *you*. It suggested that we were on the same side, not adversaries.

The editing process presents every writer with that age-old wrestling match between arrogance and humility. My initial reaction—every writer's initial reaction—is to go with the great Billy Wilder adage: "Trust your own instincts. Your mistakes may as well be your own." Yet it's also a huge mistake to not heed good advice when it's given to you.

And, being honest, I hated her because she was right. The reason I'd kept fussing with that opening line was that it didn't need to be there. In fact, it was actually *keeping* the reader from being pulled right in.

So, after gazing at it in deep reflection for several minutes, I took a deep breath, drew a line through it, and kept on going. Sat there glued to my chair, focused on Norma's editorial notes. She would leave several paragraphs alone, not mark up a single thing, but would zero in on any observation, phrase, or word that she felt wasn't as sharp as it ought it to be. She was demanding, persnickety, and annoying as hell. *We can do better* was her pet phrase. I didn't always agree with her. When I didn't, I wrote *STET* in the margin. But most of the time I had to admit she was right, and I reached for something better. It was hard work that required intense concentration. It took me three espresso-fueled hours to reach the end of chapter one, which was all of eighteen pages long.

I was in for a tough slog, but it would make the book better and that was all that mattered.

I got up and moseyed down the hall to the kitchen, Lulu eagerly leading the way despite the fact that she'd already put away a full breakfast. But she was a born optimist. Figured there was always a chance I was so wrapped up in my work that I'd forget I'd fed her. I toasted a baguette and slathered it with some of Merilee's blackberry jam from her farm in Lyme. She'd left a note on the kitchen table that said she was taking a 9:00 A.M. Ashtanga yoga class and would be back by 11:00. That morning's *New York Times,* which had been delivered to the hallway outside of our door, sat there on the table, too.

I found the story about Boyd below the fold on page three of the Metropolitan section under a typical slam-bang *Times* headline: PROMINENT LITERARY AGENT FALLS TO DEATH FROM TENTH-FLOOR TERRACE. The brief story bent over backward to be tactful but touched all the bases. Stated that Boyd Samuels, thirty-one, who until recently had been vice president of Literary Synergy for the Harmon Wright Agency, had leapt to his death from his apartment at 1330 Third Avenue yesterday at around noon. According to Alberta Pryce, the director of HWA's literary department, Samuels, a native of Cherry Hills, New Jersey, had recently been let go by HWA for undisclosed personal reasons. He had joined HWA in 1992 following the collapse of his own high-profile independent literary agency, which had represented such trouble-plagued young superstar clients as Cameron Sheffield Noyes and Delilah Moscowitz.

I had to admire the Silver Fox's class. She couldn't stand Boyd yet felt that nobody needed to know about his history of drug problems. And the details of why he'd been fired were nobody's business outside of the insular publishing world.

I strolled into the living room, gazing out the windows as I munched on my baguette. Rain was forecast for later that day, which was a good omen for my non-miracle Mets, who had unwisely signed an aging, creaky Bobby Bonilla to such a bloated contract that they barely had enough money left to sign anyone else of major-league caliber to play alongside him. It promised to be another pathetic season for suffering Met fans. But a rainout meant they wouldn't lose another game tonight, so things were looking up.

My mind strayed back to a phrase I'd just tweaked at Norma's request, wondering if I should have left it the way it was. I was starting my way back toward my office to take another look when the phone rang in the kitchen.

"Get your ass back down to Norma's office, dude!" Very barked in my ear when I answered it. "She got another one in this morning's mail. Same old-school technique—letters and words cut out of the Sunday *Times Magazine.* Mailed from the same Grand Central zip code."

"Same mucilage?"

"How did I know you were going to ask me that?"

"You would have been disappointed if I hadn't. What does this one say?"

"Just get over here, will you?"

"I'll be there as soon as I can, Lieutenant," I said into a dead phone. He'd already hung up.

◆

This time Lulu and I had to hurry to catch up with Norma's editorial assistant, Alissa, who was leading us extremely briskly toward Norma's office. Today, she wore a burgundy silk turtleneck tucked into trimly cut gabardine slacks. She had long legs and an extremely eye-worthy stride. In fact, she was eye-worthy all over. What's more, she knew she was and made sure to dress as flatteringly as possible.

I was wearing my trench coat and fedora over a navy double-breasted blazer, gray fine-waled corduroy trousers, a tattersall shirt, polka-dot bow tie, and the Gore-Tex street walkers that I'd had an elderly shoemaker on West Thirty-Second Street make for me. Lulu was wearing her

C.C. Filson duck-billed rain cap because she's susceptible to sinus problems in damp weather. Snores when her head gets stuffed up. I know this because she likes to sleep on my head.

"How are you holding up?" I asked Alissa.

She came to a halt, smiling faintly at me as she bent down to pat Lulu on the head. "It's another not-so-great day, as I take it you've heard or you wouldn't be here."

"Lieutenant Very did tell me to get my ass over here right away."

Alissa tilted her head slightly, studying me. "He seems to value your advice."

"I know. It's a distinct flaw in his character."

She let out a laugh as we resumed walking toward Norma's office. "Norma's absolutely crazy about him. I hope he doesn't break her heart."

"What makes you think he will?"

"He's a man."

"We're not all bad. Some of us are quite nice, actually."

"But he's Norma's first. She's never been in love before."

"Oh, I see. Have you?"

"Have I what?"

"Ever been in love."

"Too many times. In fact, I've stopped believing in it entirely."

"Don't do that. You're much too young to be so hard-hearted. Give it at least another full year. Actually, it so happens that before Very called me I was going to ask you if I could buy you lunch today."

Alissa flashed a dazzling smile at me. "You were? How come?"

"I like to get to know the people with whom I'll be working."

"That sounds like a wise policy. But, to be totally honest, this is probably my last week here. I've interviewed for a job as an assistant editor at Simon and Schuster and they called me last night to offer me the job."

"Congratulations."

"Thanks. I'm going to miss this place. I love it here. I love Norma. But you know the publishing business. If you stay in the same job at the same house for too long, people figure you've hit your ceiling. Got to keep moving on and up."

Alissa was savvy. Didn't mention that Norma had refused to promote her. Didn't dump on her one bit. But was she capable of sending her scary death threats as pay-back? I wondered. "I'll be sorry to see you go, but you're right. You can't stay in one place for too long."

She arched an eyebrow at me. "If we're not going to be working together, does that mean that you'll never take me to lunch?"

"I will if you'd like me to."

"Are you kidding? I don't get many invites from tall, handsome, brilliant authors."

Lulu let out a low, unhappy grumble, acutely aware that Alissa was getting flirty.

Alissa frowned. "Did I say something wrong?"

"No, she's just very protective of me."

"Does she have reason to be?"

"Twenty-four hours a day. You have my number. Give me a call when you get settled in at your new job."

"I'll do that. Or better yet . . ." We'd reached her desk outside of Norma's office. She scrawled a number on a memo pad and handed it to me. "Here's my home phone. Call me some night. I'm always up late reading—unless I get a better offer."

Subtle she was not, our Alissa.

"I'll do that," I said, tapping on Norma's door before I went in and had a look at today's death threat on her desk:

YOUR **BOYFRIEND** *can't*

SAVE **you**.

NO ONE *can*.

Her boyfriend was pacing back and forth liked a caged tiger in his same black crew-neck sweater and black jeans, his SIG tucked inside of his shoulder holster. Norma was standing by the window in another one of her shapeless knit sweaters and skirts, looking exceedingly young and tiny.

"So it's someone who has eyes on her if they know you're involved," I said to him.

"That's what I was thinking, too."

"Someone's probably just pissed off at me for rejecting their book," Norma said to him, her voice quavering slightly. "I wish you wouldn't take this so seriously. You're scaring me."

"Good. I want you to be scared," he said as I stared at the death threat. It was just as he'd told me on the phone—same old-school technique of cutout words and letters glued to a piece of copier paper. "Look all you want. Just don't touch."

"Did your people find any prints on yesterday's death threat?"

"Not a thing. It was spotless. But that doesn't mean this one is."

Lulu let out a whimper.

"What's up with her?" Very asked.

"She wants to smell it."

He donned his latex glove and held the letter in front of her so she could sniff at it carefully for a long moment before she finally moved over toward the door and stretched out, yawning.

"What, that's it?" Norma asked.

"Apparently so."

"I was expecting a little something more."

"With Lulu you never know what to expect, Coach. But, trust me, if she has something to tell us, she will. Her nose knows." I glanced at Very. "Is there any chance that the late Boyd Samuels sent this yesterday before we visited him?"

"In theory? Yes. He could have assembled it early yesterday morning, taken the subway to Grand Central, mailed it, and disposed of all the evidence before we paid our call on him. But he hardly seemed in that industrious a state, did he?"

"No, he didn't. He was sitting there in his bathrobe, totally bombed and bummed. Unless that was all an act—except we know that it wasn't or he wouldn't be in a body bag at the morgue right now. What's your plan?"

"An officer in plain clothes will be in the reception area to guard Norma all day."

"There was a tall woman in a pants suit sitting there when Lulu and I got here. She's on security detail?"

"First shift. I'll rotate them every two hours so they don't doze off. Norma has no lunch date or appointments that will take her out of the office. I'm assigning two officers in plain clothes to stay on her when she goes home."

"I'm taking the subway like I always do," she said to him defiantly. "I refuse to change my routine."

"And I'm not asking you to. I'm just playing it safe." To me he said, "Meanwhile, you, your short-legged partner, and I will start in on our most likely candidates."

Norma heaved a suffering sigh. "You're going to grill my authors?"

"*Former* authors," I said. "You lowered the boom on them, remember?"

She stuck out her lower lip. "True . . ."

"This is my job, Baby Girl," Very said. "I have to do it."

"I know," she said reluctantly. "But that doesn't mean I have to like it."

Very peered at me as he put on his dark blue NYPD rain jacket and matching baseball cap. "The reason I want you by my side is that you understand writers."

"We're not all alike, you know. Some of us pass for normal, everyday people."

"Please tell me you're not including yourself in that category. Let's go, I've got my ride parked downstairs."

"Oh, good. I've been missing those twice-weekly visits to my chiropractor." Very's battered, unmarked Crown Vic had not the slightest acquaintanceship with shock absorbers, springs, struts, or proper wheel alignment. And he drove it like a demon. Didn't avoid potholes. Sought them out. Lulu loved riding in Very's cruiser. Me? After a day spent riding shotgun, I invariably woke up with back spasms. "Who's up first?"

◆

"Thank you for seeing us, Mrs. Poole," Very said.

"No trouble at all, Lieutenant Very. I'm always happy to be of help to the NYPD. And your voice on the phone made it sound as if this might be a matter of some urgency."

"I believe it is."

"Then do come in and tell me about it."

Not that we'd had an easy time gaining access to Penelope Estes Poole's penthouse on Fifth Avenue and East Seventy-Second Street. First, we'd had to get past the white-gloved doorman in the luxuriously appointed lobby, who'd politely but firmly insisted that Very produce his shield before he would phone up to her.

"There are two gentlemen here to see you, Mrs. Poole. One of them is a Detective Lieutenant Romaine Very of the NYPD and the other is a Mr. Stewart Hoag . . . Yes, ma'am, I've examined the lieutenant's identification . . ." The doorman listened patiently before he turned to me and said, "Mrs. Poole wishes to know if you're *the* Stewart Hoag."

"I'm *a* Stewart Hoag. I don't know if I'm *the* Stewart Hoag," I said, which prompted Very to elbow me in the ribs. "Ow, that hurt."

"It was supposed to. Norma's life may be in danger, remember?"

"No offense, but you used to be a lot more fun to hang with before you fell in love."

The doorman listened to Mrs. Poole on the phone before he said to me, "She wishes to know if you are accompanied by a basset hound." He gazed over the reception desk down at Lulu, who gazed back up at him in her duck-billed cap, mouth breathing audibly. "Ma'am, I can assure you he does indeed have a basset hound with him . . . Fine . . . Very well." He hung up the phone and said, "You'll want the elevator on the far right, gentlemen. I operate it from here."

Its doors opened as we approached. It had carpeting and dark wood paneling and made only one express stop, the penthouse, where the elevator opened directly into the entry hall of a grand two-story living room, complete with a chandelier, multiple seating areas, and a stairway that curved its way up to the penthouse's second floor. A wide doorway opened into a formal dining room, which looked as if it could seat twenty-four husky eaters with plenty of elbow room. The place was so immense it made Merilee's place look like a starter apartment.

Penelope Estes Poole, the seventy-two-year-old author of thirty best-selling Weaverton Elves mysteries, crossed the vast marble-floored living room toward us. Since she had never included her photo on the dust jackets of any of her books, most of her readers—Norma included—had always assumed her to be a meek little white-haired lady. Penelope Estes Poole was anything but that. She was a tall, erect, patrician aristocrat with a long blade of a nose and the large, strong hands of an accomplished horsewoman—which indeed she was. Her chin-length hair was so expertly dyed that it gave the impression of being a natural shade of silver blond. She wore a tweed Norfolk jacket, whipcord trousers, and ankle boots. Not much in the way of jewelry. Jade earrings, a Rolex Oyster wristwatch, and her gold wedding band, which she chose to wear on her right ring finger as many widows do. Penelope must have been a striking beauty back in her Smith College days. She was still plenty handsome. And unfathomably wealthy, what with being the widowed heiress of two old-money fortunes, her own family's and that of her late husband, Harrison Poole, who'd died of a heart attack when he was only forty-eight. Penelope had never remarried or been linked romantically to another man. When she wasn't in the city she rode and bred horses on her country estate in Little Compton, an enclave in southern Rhode Island near the sound, which was so exclusive that very few ordinary New Yorkers even knew it existed. She summered at her late husband's mansion in Bar Harbor, Maine, which had served as the model for Weaverton.

"Good morning, gentlemen," Penelope said to us in a full-throated voice as I heard another set of footsteps approaching us. "Feel free to hang your hats and coats in the closet to your right."

It was a snug little closet. I doubt it could have held more than fifty mink coats.

"And now I'd like you to meet my granddaughter and unpaid literary assistant, Gretchen, without whom I'd be totally lost."

When I turned to say hello to Gretchen, I did a genuine Bud Abbott double take. Penelope's granddaughter was an astonishingly beautiful young woman. I'm talking one-in-a-million beautiful. She was slender yet shapely, with shoulder-length silky blond hair that she parted down the middle so as to frame her face. And what a face it was. Huge blue eyes, high cheekbones, creamy, flawless skin, and full, soft young lips. Gretchen's features were so perfectly sculpted that if she'd been a few inches taller, she could easily have been a top fashion model. But she stood only about five foot seven in the pumps that she was wearing with her powder-blue cashmere sweater and tan slacks. She wore no makeup or lipstick. Just a faint, delicate lemony scent. And no jewelry at all. I mean none. No rings on her delicate pink fingers. No bracelets or necklaces. No wristwatch. No earrings. Her ears weren't even pierced. Was she making some kind of statement? What statement?

"Gretchen graduated from Smith three years ago and is still trying to decide what she wants to do with her life," Penelope informed us. "She's a volunteer docent at the Metropolitan Museum of Art. She's helped renovate several buildings for Habitat for Humanity. But mostly she's helped me with my last two Elves books. I've always written them longhand. She types them into her computer for me and tidies up my prose a bit while she's at it. We've just turned in what will be our final one, *The Night of the Living Elves*. Gretchen, dear, this is Detective Lieutenant Romaine Very of the NYPD . . ."

"Pleased to meet you, Lieutenant," she said in a soft, almost girlish voice.

Very nodded to her politely, his face giving no indication whatsoever that he was the least bit conscious of her beauty.

"And this rather tall, dashing fellow is Stewart Hoag," Penelope said.

"And the short stack is Lulu," I added.

Gretchen totally ignored Lulu. Just stood there gazing up at me, wide-eyed and more than a little awestruck. "Are you . . ."

"Yes, he's *the* Stewart Hoag," Penelope said.

"Make it Hoagy."

"Forgive me, I'm just so . . . so honored to meet you, Hoagy," she said, blushing slightly. "I *loved* your first novel, *Our Family Enterprise*. The characters seemed so real to me that I felt as if I knew them. I happen to be friends with Norma's assistant, Alissa. She told me yesterday that Norma is over the moon about your new one. You must be thrilled."

"I am. It's been a long, hard struggle."

"But you didn't give up. I find that so admirable," Gretchen said before, at long last, she looked down at my partner. "And this is the famous Lulu. Hi, sweetie! Hi there!" Gretchen bent down to pet her and got her nose licked for her trouble. First, she giggled. Then she drew back, her eyes widening. "Say, her breath is . . ."

"Lulu has rather unusual eating habits."

"Nana knows a wonderful veterinary dietitian should you ever wish to consult him."

"Thank you. She's fine. Just weird."

"Yes, well, I don't believe these gentlemen came here to discuss Lulu's breath, as fascinating as the subject may be," Penelope said. "Let's move into the sitting room and get down to the reason for your visit, shall we? May I offer you coffee or anything?"

We both declined.

The sitting room, which was situated a mere half mile across the living room, was more intimate-sized, with a chintz-covered sofa and armchairs and a wood-burning fireplace that had a small fire going in it. There were framed photos of horses everywhere on the walls where there weren't framed paintings of horses.

Penelope steered me toward one of the armchairs. Very sat in the other. She and Gretchen settled on the sofa. Lulu curled up by the fire with a contented grunt.

"Do you ride?" I asked Gretchen, gazing around at all the horse art.

"Who, me? No, I'm not the outdoorsy type. Don't care for horses. Don't sail, play golf or tennis, any of those things . . ."

"Yet you must do something to stay in shape. You're very trim and fit."

She immediately blushed again. "Thank you. I have a personal trainer who comes here three mornings a week and beats the crap out of me."

Penelope studied Very with a critical eye. "I understand from Gretchen that you and Norma are romantically involved. Norma's certainly a brilliant young editor, yet for some reason I can't picture the two of you together. I suppose one can never tell about love, can one?"

"No, ma'am."

"Pardon me if I'm talking out of turn, Lieutenant, it's just that you're such a handsome young man, not to mention Dante Feldman's top homicide ace. You have a degree in astrophysics from Columbia. If you're wondering why I'm rattling on this way, the truth of it is that I'm on the lookout for a suitable young man for Gretchen."

"Nana, please!"

"Hoagy, you're of a slightly more mature age than Gretchen. Nothing wrong with that. But I understand that you and Merilee Nash are back together."

"We are."

"Are you planning to start a family?"

"Not currently."

"Take it from me, you'll be sorry if you don't. I know it's selfish of me, but I deeply regret that you're not available."

"Why is that, ma'am?"

"Because you and Gretchen would make such beautiful babies together."

Gretchen let out an exasperated sigh. "Nana, how many times have I asked you not to embarrass me this way?"

"I'm responsible for you, dear," Penelope said emphatically. "You see, gentlemen, Gretchen's father—my son, John—was killed in a yachting accident when Gretchen was seven. Her mother took off for Barbados with a fortune-hunting playboy and wanted nothing more to do with her, so I had my lawyers make sure the no-good tramp was entitled to not one penny of John's estate and have raised Gretchen myself. And now I must find her a suitable match."

"I've known her for only a few minutes," I said, "but I wouldn't think Gretchen would have much trouble meeting men."

Before Gretchen could open her mouth, Penelope said, "As it happens, she *was* engaged to a fine young man from a fine family. A Yalie, hockey player, who'd been accepted to the law school. But one Christmas break he ran off to Portugal with another fine young man from a fine family. Hasn't been heard from since."

"And after him there was Buzzy Talcott," Gretchen said, managing to inject herself into the conversation. "But I dumped him last year. Just couldn't imagine spending the rest of my life with a hedge fund trader named Buzzy, especially because he has no appreciation for the arts, no depth, no sensitivity, no sense of humor . . ."

"Aren't you being just a tiny a bit harsh, dear?" Penelope said.

Gretchen flared at her grandmother angrily. "Actually, what I was *trying* to be was *tactful*. The brutally honest truth is that Buzzy Talcott is nothing more than a complete waste of skin!"

I tugged at my ear, wondering what was behind the heat of her sudden emotional display. "Buzzy Talcott . . . Does he have an older brother named Zach?"

"Why, yes, he does. Do you know Zach?"

I nodded. "Used to play squash at the Racquet and Tennis club twice a week with him."

Gretchen looked at me in surprise. "You don't strike me as the R and T sort. It's so paleo."

"I was grandfathered in. Literally. Grandfather was a serious clubman, as was his father before him. I started going there when I first moved here from Cambridge. It seemed the inevitable thing to do, until the first time I saw the Ramones play and my life underwent a complete overhaul. I hardly go there at all anymore. So are you seeing anyone now, may I ask?"

Gretchen lowered her eyes. "Not really."

"What do you do for a social life?"

"Well, I *adore* vintage clothing," she said, brightening. "Haunt consignment shops all over town with a couple of my girlfriends. And there's this really, really fun disco-nostalgia bar on Second Avenue called Stayin' Alive. We dress up in our wide-legged, flared double-knit pants, sequined tops, and platform shoes, drink tequila sunrises, and rock out to the Bee Gees."

"That right there is the big difference between disco and punk. There is no such thing as punk nostalgia. When you're a punk, you're a punk all the way, from your first cigarette to your last dying day."

She furrowed her brow at me fetchingly. "I'm sorry, was that supposed to make sense?"

"Made sense to me," Very said. "But I've known Hoagy a lot longer than you have."

Gretchen's huge blue eyes locked onto mine and held on for an extra one, two, three seconds before she turned and gazed into the fire. "The truth is that I'm not looking to meet anyone right now. Not unless he's truly special. I have plenty to keep me busy. And it's been a privilege to help Nana with the Weaverton Elves. The Elves have been with me for my entire life. Norbert, Filbert, Noel, Virgil, Chester, Hans, Cuddles—they're like family to me. It's been a dream come true to work on these last books."

To Penelope, I said, "You must be deeply disappointed that Norma terminated the series."

"Not at all," Penelope assured me. "In fact, I'm relieved. But please don't tell anyone I said that."

"Your secret is safe with us."

"I've been grinding out a book a year every year for thirty years. I've enjoyed it immensely, mind you, but it wasn't something I planned. It started as nothing more than a lark back in the sixties when Native Son threw me in Little Compton. Damned horse broke my leg in two places. I was in a cast for months. As I had nothing else to do, and was bored stiff, I wrote a silly little story about elves for my niece, Deirdre, who was ten. She's Gretchen's aunt. Lives in Geneva, Switzerland, with her husband, Mark. He manages international funds. There is no other earthly reason to live in such a dreadfully dull city. Am I right?"

"Yes, you are," I said politely, as Lulu began snoring softly by the fire.

"My husband, Harrison, read my silly little story, thought it was 'jolly,' and sent it to a friend who was an editor at the *New Yorker* and he actually published the damned thing. Told me there's always a market for adult whimsy and suggested that the Weaverton Elves would make a terrific series of mystery novels. He ran the idea past a friend who was a literary agent. Sure enough, Guilford House signed me up, the Elves became an instant hit, and here I am, thirty books later. Writing is hard work, as I don't have to tell you, Hoagy, although trust me when I say how lucky you are that you don't write mysteries. Not only are the plots pure torture but—unlike the reader—I don't have the luxury of simply skipping over all the intricate details in the climactic scene when the Elves solve the crime. I have to make certain that the damned things actually make sense. I'm seventy-two years old and I've had it up to here with making certain that they do. The truth is that I had intended to speak to Norma about hanging up my pen, so I felt absolutely liberated when she gave me the news. I'll be able to spend more time at our family compound in Little Compton and ride as often as I want. I have a younger sister, cousins, and nephews who live there. I love being around them. I feel much lonelier here, rattling around in this huge place with Gretchen, who's always flitting about, doing this and that. But I do have to be here in the city one week a month or thereabouts because I serve on several philanthropic boards and such." She narrowed her gaze at Very. "Now, Lieutenant, would you please be kind enough to tell me the purpose of this visit?"

"Norma has received death threats in the mail the past two mornings," Very answered. "As it happens, she's had to cut ties with several authors lately. When she informed you she was pulling the plug on your Weaverton Elves series, you told her, and I quote, 'The Weaverton Elves would never allow someone like you to be happy and prosper.' "

Penelope let out a huge laugh. "And *that's* why you're here? Good gravy, I was teasing her," she said airily. "You don't think I could actually harm that brilliant young woman, do you? We're talking about fictional elves, for pity's sake. No, I was relieved when she told me, as I said." She paused, turning serious. "And I simply can't believe someone has sent the poor dear death threats."

"Of a highly old-school variety," he said grimly. "He, or she, has cut words and letters out of last Sunday's *New York Times Magazine*, glued them to a piece of copier paper with mucilage, and mailed them to her at her office from a one-zero-zero-one-seven zip code, which happens to be the location of Grand Central Terminal."

Penelope looked at him in alarm. "You're not serious."

"I assure you I am."

Penelope considered it for a moment. "Tell me, Lieutenant, who are the other authors Norma has had to cut loose?"

"One of them is Richard Groat."

Penelope nodded sympathetically. "Poor fellow. I've known him for years. A very sweet and talented man, but he's never recovered from his wife's suicide. Who else?"

"She had to shelve Professor Alexander McCord's biography of President Truman. That was a legal decision, not editorial, but it was she who gave him the news over the phone. Said it was an awful conversation."

"That comes as no surprise. He's an awful man. Not at all the kindly character that he portrays on the TV news shows."

"You don't care for him?"

"I do not. He's a fraud. Built his illustrious career by plagiarizing the work of his graduate assistants, each and every one of whom has just happened to be an attractive young woman. And he's slept with each and every one of them, of course, and has always kept it hushed up by finding them a plum academic post somewhere. I suppose one could call it a transactional arrangement. The young woman gets a good job out of it, but it's a gross abuse of his position, nonetheless. And this time it finally backfired on him. He encountered one, Scarlett Bloom, who wouldn't let him get away with it. What an odious man. He's married to Jillian Goldenson, who writes about politics for the *New Yorker.* Cheats on her every time she goes to DC."

"And you know all of this how?" Very asked.

"I serve on a financial board at Columbia University, which is taking a serious look at cutting ties with him. I'm also a major underwriter of *The MacNeil/Lehrer NewsHour.* And I have a grandniece, Dilys, who's a production assistant on the show. She told me he hits on every attractive young woman who gets within ten feet of him."

"Dilys thinks he's really gross," Gretchen said.

"To me," Penelope said, "he reeks of being a man who couldn't get a date in college and is now making up for lost time."

"Well, I think it's disgusting," Gretchen said, her smooth young cheeks blotching angrily. "How can a relationship between a man and a woman be so *transactional,* as you put it, Nana? Whatever happened to love?"

"It's still out there," I assured her. "I give you my word."

Her blue eyes locked onto mine again and didn't let go. "If you'd ever like a private guided tour of the Met, I'd be happy to take you on one."

"Why, thank you, that's very nice of you. I'd like it very much."

She produced a slim leather pouch from the hip pocket of her slacks, removed a card, and handed it to me. It was a pale gray card with nothing but her name and phone number embossed on it. "I can set it up any time. Just call me."

"Thank you. I'll do that." I glanced at Very, who was giving me a subtle nod of his head toward the door.

"And now, we'll be on our way. We've taken up enough of your time."

"Nonsense, it's been quite fascinating," Penelope said as we all stood up, Lulu stirring from her nap, and started our way across another time zone toward the elevator. "I just wish I could have been of more help."

"You were plenty helpful, ma'am," Very assured her.

"It was nice meeting you," Gretchen said to me in that soft girlish voice of hers.

I smiled at her. "Nice meeting you, too."

"You'll save my card, won't you?"

"Absolutely," I said, patting the breast pocket of my jacket as I fetched our hats and coats from the closet by the elevator.

Gretchen knelt and patted Lulu. "It was nice meeting you, too, sweetie."

Lulu responded with a low whoop and a thump of her tail.

When the penthouse express elevator arrived, we said our final goodbyes and climbed aboard, then down we went.

"Well, well . . ." I said. "If you and Norma ever hit the skids, you could step *way* up in weight class financially with that one. Plus she's some looker, too."

"Not my type," Very said curtly.

"What, rich and gorgeous?"

"Shallow. And what's with that 'Nana' shit? Makes her sound like she's seven years old."

"It's a WASP thing. Think nothing of it. So, you can discern that Gretchen's shallow from that one brief conversation?"

"I totally can. She's got no purpose or drive. Graduated from Smith, what, three years ago? And she's still trolling around for something to do besides typing her grandmother's books."

"Sounded to me as if she's been doing more than just typing them."

Very frowned at me. "Such as?"

"Making sure they were coherent. When a writer starts complaining the way Penelope was about how annoying it is that mystery climaxes are supposed to make sense, it suggests to me that hers no longer did."

"Besides, what's Gretchen doing living there with her? She should have her own place. Be independent."

When the elevator reached the lobby, the doorman opened the door for us and bid us a good day as we started toward Very's battered Crown Vic double-parked out front.

"If you could have that huge penthouse to yourself three weeks out of the month, are you telling me you wouldn't?" I asked.

"Fair point. But she's of zero interest to me. Besides, it was *you* she couldn't stop staring at."

"Not my type, either," I said, shaking my head. "She's an entitled Fifth Avenue princess, which means she's accustomed to getting whatever she wants and has zero familiarity with the word *no*. Besides, she's a major fan of the brothers Gibb. Need I say more?"

"Yeah, but she's gaga over you. I guarantee if you take her up on that private tour of the Met, you two will end up in bed together afterward in a suite at the Carlyle, which she probably owns."

Lulu immediately let out a menacing growl.

"Why's she doing that?"

"Because you're suggesting I'd cheat on Merilee and break up our happy home."

"Just thinking out loud, dude," he said as we got in his car, Lulu climbing onto the bench seat between us.

"Do me a favor. Next time you feel like thinking out loud, kindly shut up. Where to next?"

◆

We sped up Madison Avenue, spelunking our way in and out of potholes as Lulu's eyes gleamed excitedly. She loves to ride in police cars. When we reached East 110th, also known as Central Park North, Very hung a screeching left and worked his way over to the West Side, past Morningside Park and the mammoth St. John's Cathedral on Amsterdam, to Broadway. He made a right turn and we arrived in the environs of Columbia University. The formal entrance to the main campus—which I have to admit is pretty damned impressive—is the gate at College Walk, on our right at Broadway and 116th Street. But we weren't headed there. Very made a left at 116th and then a quick right onto Claremont Avenue, a ritzy little enclave of prewar high-rise apartment buildings sandwiched between Broadway and the Hudson River, where quite a few distinguished faculty members choose to live.

Alexander McCord, the renowned historian, best-selling author, TV talking head, plagiarist, and sex machine, shared a twelfth-floor apartment there with his wife, Jillian, who spent a great deal of time in Washington—which, as Penelope had mentioned, allowed McCord ample opportunity to pursue his passion for hitting on juicy young females.

A few raindrops began to fall as we got out, a hopeful sign for my Mets. McCord was expecting us. Very usually preferred to make cold calls and catch people unprepared, but he hadn't wanted to waste time showing up there only to discover that the man was on campus teaching a class.

McCord answered the door buzzer right away and helped us hang our rain gear from the hooks in the entry hall, smiling genially. "You said this was an important matter, Lieutenant Very. Naturally, I'm familiar with your reputation, so if a detective of your caliber says it's important, I'm happy to be of any assistance I can."

McCord came across in person just exactly as he did when he was on the *NewsHour*. Not pompous or condescending. A regular guy whose scholarly works were readable books for regular people. He had that familiar head of snowy white hair, a ruddy pink face, and a friendly twinkle in his eye. He was chesty and broad shouldered, but not nearly as tall as I'd expected him to be. I doubt that he was more than five foot eight. He wore a royal-blue lambswool V-neck sweater over a white oxford button-down shirt, corduroy slacks, and a pair of Timberland hiking shoes. I had zero doubt that a Harris tweed jacket with leather elbow patches completed the outfit.

He treated me to a warm smile before he said, "And you are . . . ?"

"Stewart Hoag," I said as we shook hands.

"Pleased to meet you, Stewart. Come in, come in. Please."

The apartment was cavernous, which was how they'd built them on the Upper West Side in the old days. The living room had a fireplace and its walls were lined with bookshelves. He led us down a hallway past his cluttered office. I knew it was his office because one wall featured nothing but framed copies of his book jackets. I noticed that he still wrote on an Underwood typewriter, which raised him a notch in my estimation. Jillian's office next door was equally cluttered, although she'd surrendered to a Macintosh. We made our way into a cozy sitting room with an overstuffed maroon sofa and matching armchairs. It had French doors that led out onto a terrace with a panoramic view all the way across the Hudson River to the banks of the New Jersey Palisades, which were becoming shrouded with low, dark rain clouds. Another good omen for my Mets. There were more books in the sitting room. A stereo. A butler's tray table laden with several decanters of alcohol, an ice bucket, and glasses. No television set.

Very and I sat on the sofa. McCord settled in one of the armchairs. Lulu ambled over to say hello to him, but when he did not pat her head or so much as look at her, she skulked back toward me and curled up on my feet, highly miffed. She's accustomed to being doted over.

McCord narrowed his eyes at me. "Your name sounds familiar, Mr. Hoag. Why is that?"

Very let out a laugh. "You're kidding, right? Hoagy's one of the most distinguished novelists in America."

"Ah, of course. Please forgive me. I don't read much fiction."

"When my first novel made a big splash in the early eighties, your wife, Jillian, did a profile of me for the *New Yorker*," I said.

"Is that so? We hadn't met each other yet," he said, which I happened to know.

"I remember her telling me that her true desire was to cover politics. She started spending her time in Washington soon after that."

He nodded. "Where I do a great deal of my archival research. That's where we met."

"She wrote far and away the best profile anyone has ever done of me. Spent two entire days and nights with me. Insisted I take her to all my old punk rock haunts. She even rode up to after-hours dance clubs in Spanish Harlem with me on the back of my bad black Norton. She's a terrific journalist." Terrific in the sack, too. After she'd filed her story, the two of us spent another two days and nights having wild monkey sex together. But it wouldn't have been gentlemanly of me to share that particular detail with her husband.

McCord made a steeple of his fingers, gazing at me thoughtfully. "Why, may I ask, are you here with Lieutenant Very?"

"I've found Hoagy's insights into the publishing business very helpful in the past," Very explained. "Show business, too. He lives with Merilee Nash."

McCord's eyes lit up with erectile envy. "Well, well. Clearly, you're a man worth knowing. But, tell me, why have you brought your dog with you?" he asked, acknowledging Lulu's presence for the first time.

"Lulu's my partner. We're like Gunther Toody and Francis Muldoon."

He peered at me quizzically. "Sorry, I don't take the reference."

"I gather you weren't a big fan of *Car 54, Where Are You?*"

"Actually, I don't believe I've ever heard of it. But my field is the American presidency, not its junk culture."

"We're going to pretend we didn't hear that," I said, as Lulu joined in with a sour grumble. She loves Toody and Muldoon.

McCord glanced at his watch. "I have a faculty meeting at the top of the hour. So we'd best hurry this along. How may I help you, Lieutenant?"

"Norma Fives, your former editor, received death threats in the mail yesterday and today. I'm obliged to touch base with any authors who've had run-ins with her recently."

"That'll keep you busy for quite some time. She's a total bitch."

"Before you dig yourself into a deeper hole," I said, "I should tell you that Lieutenant Very and Norma live together."

McCord's pink cheeks reddened. "Oh, dear. I apologize, Lieutenant. Please forgive me."

Very didn't. Just glared at him. "After Norma informed you in a conference call that your Truman biography had been dropped due to the plagiarism suit filed against you by your former graduate assistant, Scarlett Bloom, I'm told that you were highly abusive toward her on the phone. Hollered, screamed, called her all sorts of names—even though you knew perfectly well that it was the publisher's lawyers who'd made the decision, not Norma."

McCord gazed out the French doors. The rain was now starting to fall lightly but steadily, and what a lovely rain it was. "You're absolutely right, Lieutenant," he conceded. "I lost my temper, and I owe her an apology. It's just that I'm so incredibly proud of the book. I think it's the best work of my career. And this plagiarism nonsense, and I do mean nonsense, has destroyed my reputation—all because Scarlett is trying to punish me for something that happened several years ago."

"By which you mean you two were romantically involved," I said.

He let out a pained sigh. "A bit of hero worship on her part that I allowed to go too far. I showed poor judgment. Jillian was away in Washington quite a bit. And Scarlett is a very attractive young woman. Surely you can understand. We're all men here."

Lulu let out a whimper of protest.

McCord studied her curiously. "I would swear your dog understands every word I'm saying, which puts her ahead of half of my lecture students."

"She does understand every word you're saying—as long as you don't say it in French."

"And why is that?"

"She doesn't speak French."

He peered at me, mystified. "You're a rather strange person, aren't you?"

"Strange? No, I don't think so. But I am an acquired taste."

"I see." He fell silent for a moment. "I acted inappropriately with Scarlett. When I realized that the proper thing to do was break it off with her, she got very upset, even though I wrote her a glowing recommendation that landed her a tenure-track position at Duke."

"Did you tell Jillian about it?" I asked.

"I did. We had a frank conversation. She was deeply hurt, as you might imagine, but we worked our way through it—although this flare-up over the Truman biography has brought it all into the public eye, so she's not very pleased with me right now. And, needless to say, I'm furious with Scarlett, who had a promising academic career ahead of her. Filing this plagiarism suit against me will do nothing but hurt her, because she has no proof. Not a bit."

"The Guilford House lawyers seem to think she does," Very said.

"That's because they're frightened rabbits. My own lawyers will prove that I did not plagiarize her thesis. I did exactly what I've been doing for the past thirty-two years—my own solid scholarship. I'm sure another publisher will agree with me. My book *will* get published and my reputation *will* be restored."

I tugged at my ear. "You said you showed poor judgment when you got romantically involved with Scarlett. Yet you've continued to have affairs with other attractive young women."

He brushed some invisible crumbs from his thigh. "That's an utterly baseless accusation."

"Really? So you didn't have an affair with Norma's assistant, Alissa?"

He fell into defeated silence. "She . . . told you about us?"

"No, you did."

"*I* did? When?"

"Just now."

"Think you're pretty smart, don't you?" he said accusingly.

"Not particularly. But I can say without reservation that you're not. Just a horny middle-aged married man who seduces younger women and tosses them aside."

"Alissa slept with me because she was hoping I could help her find a better job at another publishing house. I slept with her because she has beautiful legs."

"Does Jillian know about her, too?"

"What my wife does or doesn't know about is not any of your business."

"What would happen if she found out? Would she be as forgiving this time?"

"I repeat, it's not any of your business." He turned to Very and said, "Lieutenant, I thought you were here to talk about the death threats that Norma has been receiving in the mail."

"We are."

"Do you honestly think that I would do something that juvenile? It's preposterous. If I *were* planning to kill Norma—which, allow me to assure you, I have no intention of doing—I wouldn't waste my time sending her threatening letters. I'd simply follow her from the office after work, shove her in front of a moving city bus, and be done with it." He glanced at his watch. "Now if you gentlemen will excuse me, I have a meeting to attend."

"Of course," Very said. "Thank you for your time."

McCord led us out through the living room to the vestibule. He opened the apartment door while we put our rain gear back on. "I doubt I can be of any further help to you, Lieutenant, but feel free to call on me again if you think I can be. I would just ask you not to bring this man and his dog with you," he said, glaring at me with such intense animosity that I decided to be careful around moving city buses in the days and nights to come.

And with that he closed the door in our faces quite firmly. Didn't slam it, but almost.

"Nice guy," I said, as we started toward the elevator.

"A real sweetheart." Very popped a fresh piece of bubble gum in his mouth. "But I don't think he sent Norma those death threats."

"I don't, either. I think he mouthed off on the phone and got it out of his system, same as Boyd—although I don't see him jumping off his terrace right now. Not with that ego."

"I sure hope you're right. Two Brodies in two days would be a bit much."

We rode the elevator down, made our way out of the lobby, and stood under the awning. The rain was now falling steadily. What a glorious day to be a Mets fan.

"I have to stop in at the house and explain to my captain what I've been doing for the past two days," Very said, his jaw working on his gum.

By *the house* he was referring to the Twenty-Fourth Precinct on West One Hundredth Street.

"Fair enough. I've got some business to take care of myself."

"Which is what exactly?"

"Lieutenant, you pulled me away from my manuscript and asked for my help, remember?"

"What's *that* supposed to mean?"

"It means don't crowd me. Let me work my side of the street, okay?"

His head started nodding to its own rock 'n' roll beat. "I don't like the idea of not knowing what you're doing."

"Fine. In that case I'll go back to work on my manuscript instead."

"Aw, hell, forget I said that, dude. I'm just worried about my girl."

"I know you are."

"Will you still be on the Upper West Side when you're done working your so-called side of the street?"

"Yes, I will be."

He pulled a small memo pad from the chest pocket of his NYPD rain jacket and opened it, his eyes scanning his notes. "Next up is Richard Groat, the gentleman-thief novelist. He lives at Four Ninety-Eight West End Avenue, near West Eighty-Fourth Street. Since he suffers from such acute anxiety that he's afraid to go outside, there's a pretty decent chance he'll be home. Can you meet me there at, say, four o'clock?"

"I can."

Very stayed put under the awning. Took off his NYPD baseball cap and ran a hand through his thick black hair. "I don't want to lose her, dude."

I patted him on the shoulder, which was like making contact with a small granite boulder. "I know you don't, but if it makes you feel any better, allow me to assure you that all writers are basically cowards. If we had the courage to act on our convictions, then we'd act on them, not sit in an empty room all day writing about them."

"Meaning?"

"Meaning these letters are empty threats, nothing more."

"No, they're not," he said with total certainty.

"How do you know that?"

"Because it's my job to know it. This is what I get paid to do for a living, remember? And I'm good at my job. And right now I'm totally freaking out."

CHAPTER FIVE

I love to walk the streets of New York in the rain wearing my trench coat and fedora, its brim turned low, my hands in my pockets. On rainy days the city becomes so many different shades of slate gray that it's transformed back into a film noir from the forties. And I become Robert Mitchum, except with a better vocabulary. Lulu loves it, too, especially if she's got her duck-billed rain hat on to keep her head dry. She's made for the rain. Her oily coat repels water and keeps her from getting soaked.

Scotty's diner anchored a run-down five-story building on the corner of Broadway and West 102nd. Scotty's was open twenty-four hours a day, which made it a popular destination for cab drivers. Next door was Pearl's Nails. The second floor was occupied, according to the lettering in the picture window, by the Sylvan Ornstein Insurance Agency, Home and Auto. The top three floors of the building were apartments. Cheap apartments.

Madonna's insipid new hit, "Take a Bow," was blaring away on Scotty's sound system when Lulu and I walked in. Norma's big sister, Amy, absolutely adored Madonna. We'd had a running feud over her for years, as in I would give Amy grief over her musical taste, or total lack thereof, and Amy would invite me to fuck off.

The lunch crowd had cleared out by now and there were only a few people hunched over coffee at the counter. I hung my wet trench coat, my fedora, and Lulu's cap by the door. Lulu's rain-dampened coat immediately began to give off a strong, oily odor, which is something you'll have to get used to if you ever want to cohabitate with a basset.

Amy's face lit up when she got sight of us. "It's LULU!" she cried out, bustling her way excitedly around the counter in her waitress uniform and sneakers.

"Hey, I'm here, too, you know," I pointed out.

"My God, Hoagy, I thought the two of you had dropped off the face of the earth." She threw me into a bear hug and didn't let go. Amy Fives looked nothing like her scrawny, bony-nosed kid sister. She was about five foot six, hippy, bosomy, and big bottomed. Not exactly fat but definitely a good-sized load of a woman, with frizzy black hair and heavy-lidded brown eyes. Her nose was thick. Her lips were thick. It was hard to believe that the two of them were related. "You used to come in here *every* day for tuna melts. And then you totally disappeared."

"We moved to the high-rent district," I said when she finally released me.

Her dark eyes widened. "Don't tell me you and Merilee are back together . . ."

"Okay, I won't."

"Oh, I'm so happy for you! In fact, just to show you how happy, I'll even turn off Madonna." She reached behind the counter and flicked off the music, then got down on her knees to devote her full attention to Lulu. "Come here, you little sweetie," she cooed, scrunching Lulu's ears. Lulu let out a low, happy whoop. Amy was just about to give her a hug when she drew back, crinkling her nose. "Oh, damn, I forgot. She smells just like cod-liver oil when she gets wet. We better dry her off or everyone in the place will clear out. Take her in the men's room and close the door. I'll grab some towels."

Lulu and I did as we were told. Amy was not to be messed with. She barged in a moment later and closed the door behind her, then the two of us knelt and rubbed Lulu with dish towels while Lulu wriggled around in pure pleasure.

"Oh, you're just the cutest," Amy said to her as she rubbed her dry. "If your daddy's not careful, I'm going to smuggle you home."

After we'd done our best, we both washed our hands thoroughly to get the smell out, and then I took a booth by the window, Lulu curling up eagerly at my feet. She'd missed her Scotty's tuna melts. Amy called out an order to Scotty for two of them, minus the toast on one. Then she came over and poured me a steaming hot cup of coffee. I took a grateful sip, gazing out the window at the rain. Since Amy had no other customers at the moment, she grabbed herself a cup of coffee and joined us, beaming at me.

"Do I dare ask you how the writing's going?"

"You may not only dare but you'd better prepare yourself for one hell of a shock. I just sold my new novel for big bucks."

"Oh, sweetie, that's great! You fought so hard for years and years. Never gave up. Never stopped believing. You're my idol. Who bought it?"

"That's the truly crazy part. Norma—who, hello, I had no idea was your sister—is my new editor."

A look of dismay flashed across Amy's face and then was gone, but it had been there. "So you're going to be published by the Mouse?"

I blinked at her in surprise. "That's what you call her—the Mouse?"

"Hell yeah. Ever since we were kids." Amy shook her head in amazement. "I can't believe you two'll be working together."

"And it's a real coup, let me tell you. She's the hottest editor in town."

Scotty rang a bell, which meant our tuna melts were ready. Amy got up and returned with them. Lulu immediately went to work devouring hers. I was a bit more genteel attacking mine, but not a whole lot. It was damned good. There was just something about the way Scotty made them. Maybe it was the tons of extra-sharp cheddar.

Amy watched me eat. "Still the best in town?"

"The best," I assured her between bites.

"So how is the Mouse? She still dating that homicide detective?"

"They're living together now, actually."

"Well, that's good."

"But she's not doing so well. Anything but, in fact. Someone has been sending her death threats."

"I can't say I'm surprised," Amy said, calmly sipping her coffee.

I swallowed. "You're not? Why do you say that?"

"The Mouse has a way of pissing people off. I ought to know. I grew up in the same house with her. All the girls in school hated her. It was like she went out of her way to antagonize them. She'd boast about how much smarter she was than they were. How she was going to be a big success in life and they weren't. She had contempt for them. Contempt for me, too. The two of us never got along." Amy took another sip of her coffee. "At home, she was the golden child. Straight-A student who got a scholarship to a fancy college. Our folks showered her with attention and love. Me, they totally ignored. I was just the lumpy C-minus student who smoked cigarettes behind the auditorium and was crazy about boys. Which the Mouse wasn't. She never went out on a date. Not once. All she ever did was study. And now she's the editor in chief of a major publishing house and I'm the dummy who slings sandwiches. But I'm cool with it."

Lulu finished devouring her lunch and licked her chops before she climbed into the booth next to Amy, resting her head in her lap. Amy stroked her affectionately.

"You're not dumb, Amy. There are all different sorts of intelligence."

She let out a laugh. "Is that right? What sort do I have?"

"You can read people. The things you were just telling me about Norma? They were real insightful."

"I wouldn't know about that. All I know is I got no ambition. Scotty's going to retire soon and wants me to take over the place. I keep telling him no. My Manny thinks I should, but I don't want the responsibility. I'm cool just waiting on tables. I got my apartment in Washington Heights. And I got my Manny."

"So the two of you are still happy together?"

"Definitely."

"You don't worry about him driving around in dangerous neighborhoods late at night?"

"Nah. He can take care of himself. Besides, he's got protection."

I polished off my own sandwich, wiping my fingers on a napkin. "He carries a gun?"

"You didn't hear that from me."

Manny was a Puerto Rican–born cabbie in his early forties who used to stop in at Scotty's two or three times on his overnight shift to get coffee. Eventually, he started making those stops to see Amy. Manny had a wife and two kids in Puerto Rico to whom he sent money, and he was, supposedly, bunking with his younger brother, Raoul, in the Lincoln projects in East Harlem. But he mostly lived with Amy.

"Hoagy, he's the sweetest guy I've ever been with. We have great sex. We watch stupid movies together and laugh a lot. I think we've seen *Ghostbusters,* like, ten times. I know our thing's never going anywhere, what with him having a family back home, but I'm cool with that, too." She narrowed her gaze at me. "These death threats the Mouse is getting. Are they serious?"

"Her boyfriend seems to think so."

"He have any idea who might be sending them?"

"A few candidates. She's had to lay off some authors lately. She also got a top literary agent fired for being a sleazy liar who totally hosed her. But him we can cross off the list. He jumped off his tenth-floor balcony yesterday."

"She got him fired him and he *killed* himself? Jeez . . ."

"So I take it you and Norma don't stay in close touch?"

"You mean like normal sisters who jabber on the phone every day, go shopping together, and meet for lunch and stuff? No, we're not like that. We never talk on the phone. And she never stops by here to see me. I'm a diner waitress in a crummy neighborhood. I live with a married Puerto Rican cabbie. I'm an embarrassment to her."

An elderly couple came in and sat down in a vacant booth. Amy got up, fetched the coffeepot, and poured each of them a cup, chatting away, super friendly. After she'd given their orders to Scotty, she sat back down with us. Lulu immediately put her head back in her lap.

"Damn, Hoagy, it's good to see the two of you. I missed you."

"I forgot how good it is to be here. We'll be back. Tell me something, do you resent her?"

"Who, the Mouse? I guess I did back when we were kids. But I outgrew that years ago. Besides, looking back on it now, I was the one who was happy, not her. I had lots of friends. We'd cut class and get high. Go to movies. Make out with boys. We had fun. The Mouse never had fun. All she ever did was sit alone in her room reading. Never had a single friend. I mean, like, ever. You know what the other girls used to call her? Little Miss Strange."

A cab slowed to a halt outside in a no-parking zone and out into the rain climbed a middle-aged guy in an olive-drab fatigue jacket, jeans, and work boots, who was built like a refrigerator with arms and legs.

"There's my Manny now," Amy said, her face lighting up as she got up to greet him. "He always stops by for his coffee and kiss before his shift."

Manny took a last drag on the cigarette he was smoking, flicked it aside, and made his way inside with a big grin on his moon-shaped face. "How's my sweet thing?"

"Just fine now, babe."

She gave him a kiss and poured him a coffee to go.

"Extra sugar, okay? For some reason I got no energy today."

"Maybe because you got no sleep last night, you animal," she teased him.

"One of us is an animal, but it ain't me." He glanced over in my direction, his chin stuck out slightly. "Who's that fancy gee you're sitting with?"

"That's Stewart Hoag, the famous author. I've told you about him. Used to come in all the time with his basset hound, Lulu, for tuna melts when he lived in the neighborhood after his ex-wife, Merilee Nash—*the* Merilee Nash—gave him the boot."

"Oh, sure," he said, nodding his head.

"But they're back together now so I haven't seen him for ages. He stopped by because he and Lulu missed Scotty's tuna melts. Come say hi."

He made his way down the aisle toward us. "Manny Rojas, bro. Glad to know ya."

"Likewise," I said, shaking his big, meaty hand. "All I've been hearing about since I got here is how happy you make Amy."

He let out a rumble of a laugh. "Well, that goes both ways."

"Hey, get this," Amy said, elbowing him. "The Mouse is going to publish Hoagy's new book. How about that, hunh?"

"Hey, that's great, bro. Congratulations."

"Thank you."

"So this is Lulu, hunh? She's a cutie." He scrunched her ears. "We got to get us one."

Amy peered out the rain-smeared window. "Hey, a cop just pulled up behind your cab."

"Damn, he'll give me a ticket if I don't scoot. Love you, babe. And nice meeting you, bro." Manny hurried out into the rain. "Okay, okay, keep your shirt on!" he yelled to the cop, who cut him some slack and moved along. Grinning, Manny climbed back in his cab, blew Amy a kiss, and drove off.

"That's my Manny," she said with a lovestruck grin on her face.

"Seems like a real happy guy."

"That he is. And I know how to make him happy." Scotty called to her that her order was ready. She brought the elderly couple their sandwiches, chatting with them briefly. Then she returned to Lulu and me. "What were we talking about?"

"Norma. Whether or not you bear any kind of a grudge."

"Oh, right. Nah. I don't have any feelings about the Mouse one way or the other. Being honest, I don't even think of her as my sister anymore."

"What do you think of her as?"

"A total stranger."

◆

The rain let up as Lulu and I strolled down Broadway, which was most definitely not a good omen for my New York Mets. As we walked, I found myself pondering what Amy had said to me about Norma. Had she been honest about harboring no ill will toward her publishing wunderkind of a sister? She'd certainly sounded sincere. Seemed perfectly content with her own life, and with Manny. Was it possible that she really, truly didn't give a damn about Norma? Sure, it was.

All except for the part where I wasn't buying one word of it.

The Loews quadruplex on Broadway and West Eighty-Fourth Street was showcasing *Bad Boys,* with Martin Lawrence and Will Smith, *Tommy Boy,* with Chris Farley and David Spade, *While You Were Sleeping,* a Sandra Bullock would-be romantic comedy, and *Pulp Fiction,* from that visionary directorial genius Quentin Tarantino,

Hollywood's latest, hottest rip-off artist and schlock-meister. With each passing year, I keep getting the feeling that Hollywood is turning itself into a recycling center, regurgitating movies that have already been made before in decades past by better directors, actors, and writers.

It's starting to make me feel crazy and old before my time.

We crossed Broadway and moseyed over to West End, where I spotted Very's cruiser illegally double-parked. The man himself was pacing impatiently in front of the high-rise prewar building that was home to novelist Richard Groat, author of the best-selling series about a supremely clever gentleman thief named Mooney. Groat had been an Edgar Award–winning master until suffering his total breakdown after his wife's suicide.

And so, Norma had been forced to lower the boom on him.

"How's it going?" I asked Very, taking note of how viciously his jaw was attacking his bubble gum.

"My captain thinks I'm letting my personal feelings for Norma cloud my professional judgment is how it's going," he fumed at me, pacing, pacing. "He said that a couple of death threats from a pissed-off writer don't merit a homicide investigation. As a personal favor, he's giving me until the end of the day before I go back to catching quote, unquote *real* cases. I told him that Boyd Samuels is quote, unquote *really* dead and he told me I handle homicides, not suicides. So I said, 'Hey, what if they're connected? What if Boyd's the one who sent Norma the death threats?' And do you want to know what my oh-so-wise captain said to me?"

"I can't wait to hear."

"He said, 'If that's how it went down, then the case is already closed and you're wasting the taxpayers' money.' I had no comeback, dude. Just stood there with my mouth open like a total jerk. But consider me schooled. I should never, ever work a case where I'm personally involved with the potential victim. Clearly, I'm not scoring any points."

"You will, Lieutenant. I have total faith in you."

Lulu let out a low whoop.

"And so does the short stack."

"Thanks, I appreciate it. Not feeling real proud of myself right now."

"Try to put it behind you. We're moving on now."

"Right, right. We're moving on."

Richard Groat's building didn't have a doorman, just a vestibule with buzzers and two elevators. It was a fourteen-story building. Four apartments to a floor except for the penthouse floor, which had two apartments. Groat had one of those.

"Think he'll let us in?" I asked.

"I know he will. I phoned him before I drove over here. The guy suffers from such acute anxiety I was afraid that if I didn't give him a heads-up, he'd bolt the door and yell at us to go away. But he promised me he'd see us."

Very buzzed apartment 14A. A voice answered. Very identified himself, and, sure enough, Groat buzzed us in. We rode the elevator up, Very's knee jiggling impatiently.

When the elevator door opened, there was a small hallway with two doors. The door to 14A was open and Richard Groat stood there in the doorway waiting for us, dressed in a gray sweatshirt with the sleeves cut off at his shoulders, sweatpants, and Adidas sneakers. He was close to sixty years old but in incredible shape. His exposed biceps and forearms bulged with muscle. His stomach was flat, his posture erect. But he trembled visibly as he stood there. He also blinked a lot. The poor man looked terrified. He stood about five foot ten, with salt-and-pepper hair, deep-set brown eyes, and a two-day growth of beard.

"Nice to meet you, Lieutenant," he said in a quavering voice.

"Likewise, Mr. Groat. This is Stewart Hoag, who helps me out sometimes with cases of a literary bent."

He blinked at me, swallowing. "This . . . is a real honor for me. I'm a huge fan."

"That's kind of you to say. It's mutual. I've gobbled up everything you've ever written. You have an incredibly nimble mind."

"Thank you," he responded faintly, lowering his gaze. "And this must be the famous Lulu."

"No, I got rid of Lulu. Too much trouble. This is Hermione, who requires much less maintenance."

Groat looked at me blankly.

"I was just joshing you. It's Her Earness, all right. The one and only."

He bent over and patted Lulu gently on the head. "Sorry, I—I'm a bit slow on the uptake. I don't talk to many people anymore. I'm prone to panic attacks, you see. Never know when they'll hit, which makes me terrified to go outside. I only leave this apartment to visit my psychiatrist three mornings a week. Happily, he has a ground-floor office two buildings away from here, although for me it's like crossing the Sahara. In addition to our talk therapy, he has me on a cocktail of antianxiety meds that allow me to cope. I'm also allowed a half bottle of Chianti with dinner. I manage," he said to us as we continued to stand there in the doorway. "I have my groceries and wine delivered. Buy my clothing mail order. My lawyer, Saul Tucker, has his secretary handle mailing my bills. I leave them in an envelope outside of the door for her. She also deposits my royalty checks, withdraws cash for me, and . . ." He trailed off, an aghast expression on his face. "I forgot to invite you in. I'm still making you lurk out here in the hall. I'm so sorry!"

I said, "Not to worry. We're accustomed to lurking in hallways. Isn't that right, Lieutenant?"

"Totally. Hallways are just about our favorite places to lurk."

"You're both being incredibly kind. Come in, please."

Groat's living room was spacious. It needed to be. It was filled with so much exercise equipment it practically looked like a health club. He'd installed nearly a dozen Nautilus weight machines, an inversion table, a rowing machine, and an exercise bike. In lieu of carpeting he had blue gym-mat flooring. Large windows looked out over Riverside Park a block away and, in the distance, the Hudson. They were new windows—the kind you find in office towers, which can't be opened. I suspect he'd put them in after his wife's suicide to keep himself from pulling a Boyd Samuels.

"How many hours a day do you work out?" Very asked him.

"Two. I never miss a day. It holds me together. Without my exercise and my meds, I'd have to live in a hospital for crazy people."

No wall separated the living room from the kitchen. Just a counter on which there was a six-pack of plastic mineral-water bottles and a tray filled with so many different kinds of prescription pill bottles that I lost count. The kitchen was huge and looked as if it had been designed for a gourmet chef, complete with an extensive collection of cookbooks. Groat's office was in an alcove off the living room. There were no papers on his desk, and his IBM Selectric had a plastic cover on it, as if it had been put to sleep.

Groat's gaze followed mine. "I have no more ideas for capers. My head used to be bursting with them, but that was because of Glenda. My wife was my inspiration. When she took her life, I lost all interest in writing."

He led us into a comfy den with two cocoa-brown corduroy sofas and matching easy chairs, a TV, and bookshelves filled with a library of videocassettes. Hardly any books, although he did have a shelf reserved for his own books and his Edgar statue. A lobby poster of the hit Michael Caine–Cher movie based on his novel *Hot Locks* adorned one wall.

He stood there uneasily, wringing his hands. "May I offer you fellows a glass of carrot juice? I make it myself."

We both declined. His hand shook as he poured himself some and invited us to have a seat. We sat on one of the sofas. Lulu sprawled out on the floor at my feet with that groan she makes that sounds like a basketball deflating.

I studied the shelf of his books. "I'm genuinely sorry there won't be any new Richard Groats."

He perched on the edge of the sofa, facing us. "And I'm genuinely sorry to disappoint you, but I just don't have it in me anymore. That's what I told Norma when she showed up here to tell me she was cutting me loose."

"You also told her she'd regret it," Very pointed out.

Groat nodded. "She will."

"That could be taken as a threat."

Groat raised his eyebrows in surprise. "A threat? Oh no, no, no. I simply meant that she'd feel badly about it in the weeks to come. A job like hers forces people to perform many unpleasant tasks. Norma pretends that she's tough as nails, but she isn't. She's a sensitive young woman. I—I was sympathizing with her."

Very studied Groat curiously. "You said that you leave an envelope for your lawyer's secretary outside of the door. Does she ever come inside?"

"No, never."

He gazed around. "Who cleans the place?"

"I do. I'm very thorough. I wipe down the exercise equipment with an antibacterial spray after every workout. I vacuum. Mop the kitchen and bathrooms. Scrub the toilets. Wax the furniture. Polish the silver. I had a washer-dryer installed in one of the guest bedrooms so I can do all my own laundry. I've also become an excellent chef, if I do say so myself. I make a gourmet dinner every evening, sit down in here with my TV tray, and choose a favorite classic movie to watch. Lately, I've fallen back in love with The Saint movies with George Sanders. I've always thought his portrayal of Simon Templar was more faithful to the Leslie Charteris novels than Roger Moore's in that British TV series back in the sixties, which was frivolous and—and . . ." Groat trailed off. "Sorry, I took two milligrams of Xanax before you arrived. I'm starting to babble, aren't I?"

"Don't sweat it," Very said. "You must get lonely being here by yourself all the time. Forgive me for being personal, but what do you do for female companionship?"

Groat blinked at him. "Sex, you mean? Interesting that you should ask. As it happens, the more physically fit I became, the more it turned into an issue. Leading a totally celibate life, that is to say. I finally broke down and mentioned it to Saul. We have no secrets from each other. I've known him for thirty years. We went to NYU law school together."

"I didn't know you were a lawyer," I said.

"I'm not. Never practiced. Never took the bar exam. But sometimes you have to really sink your teeth into something to find out that it's not what you want to do with your life."

"I hear you," Very said. "I have a degree in astrophysics and look what I ended up doing."

"So what did Saul say?"

"He said, 'I'll take care of it.' "

"Take care of it, as in . . ."

"One of his clients is a highly professional, highly discreet woman whose profession is providing solutions to situations such as mine."

"She's a madam, in other words," Very said.

"Well, yes," Groat acknowledged, wringing his hands nervously again. "But Saul assured me she was *the* most elite, trustworthy madam in New York City and that she vets her girls extremely carefully. They not only look like fashion models but are well-bred and extremely intelligent. They have to be. Their services cost fifteen hundred dollars per night. At first, I was highly reluctant, but Saul talked me into it. He thought it would be a healthy step for me. He even insisted on picking up the tab for my first night. And it . . . well, it has led to quite an adventure, I must confess." He finished his carrot juice and fell silent after that.

"You're not just going to leave us hanging in suspense, are you?" I asked him.

"Come on, tell us more," Very urged him. "What was the girl's name?"

"Her name was, and is, Lola Lux. Lola's been staying with me two, sometimes three, nights a week for more than a year now. Lola and no one else."

Very nodded slowly. "And what's her real name? Her nonprofessional name, I mean."

Groat blinked at him. "Her name is Lola."

"Does she wear yellow feathers in her hair and a dress cut down to there?" On Groat's utterly blank look, I said, "That's okay, I'm not a big Barry Manilow fan, either. Please, continue."

He breathed in and out raggedly, wringing his hands yet again. "The first night she showed up, I felt like a—a sweaty teenaged boy. I—I couldn't believe how lovely a young woman she was. Tall, slim, and graceful, with long black hair and beautiful brown eyes. She was fashionably dressed, extremely well spoken. She told me she was Canadian. Came to New York all the way from Winnipeg to try to make a career for herself as a fashion model."

"Did she have a Canadian accent?" Very asked.

"Not that I noticed. They often don't in the Western provinces, especially younger people. But I wasn't paying close attention to her accent, I must confess. I was preoccupied by the way she crossed and uncrossed her legs. She was wearing a short skirt, and her legs were exceptional. I can still remember the first dinner I made for us," he recalled fondly. "Veal piccata, whipped potatoes, and sautéed spinach with an excellent bottle of Chianti Classico. For dessert I made chocolate mousse."

"What did the two of you talk about?" I asked.

"Glenda, mostly," Groat confessed. "How much trouble I was having getting past her suicide. How my writing had tapered off to, well, nothing. I showed her my shelf of books. She was thrilled to meet a successful author. Never had before. After dinner I washed and dried the dishes. She wanted to help but I wouldn't let her, since she was my guest."

Very let out an impatient sigh. "Dude, she wasn't your guest. You were paying her to get naked with you. So did you go to bed with her?"

"I—I did," Groat replied. "And she was more than willing to have sex with me. But I wasn't ready yet. She was a total stranger. She could tell that it was too soon for me, so she just let me enjoy cuddling with her and stroking her. I'd missed having physical contact with a woman, especially one so young who had such smooth skin. But that's all we did. I fell asleep with her resting her head on my chest and when I woke up the next morning, she was still right there, fast asleep, feeling safe and snug. When I stirred, she woke up and smiled at me contentedly. I made us big cups of cappuccino and climbed back into bed with her. After we drank them, she said, 'I swear, you're the sweetest man I've ever met.' That was when I kissed her for the first time, and before I knew it we were screwing each other's brains out. She was incredibly enthusiastic and inventive. She . . . did things that Glenda never did. At some point I got up and made us omelets and we ate them in bed, giggling at each other. I put the dishes in the sink and came back to bed, then we dozed for a while but it wasn't long before we were going at it again. We couldn't get enough of each other. And we've been seeing each other ever since."

"This started a year ago, you said?" Very asked,

"Yes. After a few weeks she asked me to stop paying her, because she no longer thought of me as a client. We worked out together on my exercise equipment. She does her homework here—she started taking a class in American lit at the New School. Her idea, not mine. She's reading *On the Road* right now. She keeps some clothes here. Keeps telling me I'm the world's nicest guy and that the sex with me is the best she's ever had. I've been writing about con artists half of my life. I know exactly what you're going to say next—that she's working me for some sort of scam. But she hasn't asked me for a thing yet. Not to loan her money for her mother's heart surgery. Or to invest in a health spa in Soho. If she's working me, she's being damned clever about it because she still hasn't made her play."

"What will you do if she does?" I asked.

Groat's face fell. "Drop her in a second, with profound regret."

"Does Lola have her own key to this apartment?" Very asked.

"No, never."

"Why not?"

"She's a call girl, remember? I have no idea who her friends are. She could get a copy of the key made and one of them could show up here some night when I'm alone, tie me up, and rob me. I may have crippling anxiety issues, but stupid I'm not."

"Does she still see other clients?"

He let out an exasperated sigh. "Forgive my asking, Lieutenant, but why are you so obsessed with her?"

"Just answer the question, please."

"I assume she does, since she's no longer getting any money from me. But I don't ask and she doesn't tell. All I care about is that this is the first pleasurable relationship I've had since Glenda died. I'm enjoying it while I can. If it has to end, so be it."

"You surprise me," I said to him. "One minute you sound like a lovestruck schoolboy, the next minute you're prepared to slam the door in Lola's face without hesitation."

Groat said nothing to that. Just sat there, blinking.

Very said, "Were you being straight with us when you said you don't know what her real name is?"

"Why does that matter?"

"You tell me what it is and I'll tell you why it does."

Groat hesitated. "It's Donkin. Jean Donkin."

Very jotted it down in his notepad. "Doesn't exactly roll off the tongue the same as Lola Lux, does it? The reason I asked you for her real name is so that I can run a criminal background check on her."

Groat suddenly began to shudder uncontrollably, which signaled that a panic attack was on its way. Trust me, I've been there. He scrambled hurriedly to his feet, fetched one, two, three pills from his meds tray and swallowed them with several gulps of water before he started his way back to his chair, making a huge effort to breathe slowly and deeply, in and out, in and out. He sat, continuing to breathe in and out. "You . . . think she might have a criminal record?"

"Or possibly a history of associating with known criminals." Very studied him curiously. "Forgive me, but I don't understand why you're freaking out this way. You're no babe in the woods. You said so yourself."

"Because I don't want to lose her!" he cried out. "I *need* her!"

"Perfectly understandable," I said soothingly. "She means a lot to you."

"She does! Tell me, Lieutenant, what do you hope to gain by finding out if she has a criminal background?"

"In my experience you never know where a thread might lead you. In this particular case, it might bring us to the reason why we're here."

"Why *are* you here?" he demanded, continuing to breathe deeply in and out as he slowly calmed himself. "Why are we having this conversation?"

"Because someone has started mailing Norma Fives death threats."

Groat's eyes widened in surprise. "Oh, that poor young woman. What do these threats say?"

"The first one said, 'Say goodbye. You are a dead woman. This is no joke.' The second one said, 'Your boyfriend can't save you. No one can.' "

"Why would her boyfriend be a factor?"

"Because that would be me."

Groat brightened. "*You're* dating Norma? I had no idea. Well, I'm happy for both of you. Now I understand why you were so keenly interested that I told her 'You'll regret this.' But it's not me, Lieutenant. I haven't been writing them. I'm not a writer anymore. Not even of death threats."

"You really don't think you'll feel the urge to pick it up again?" I asked him.

"I'm positive I won't. For one thing, I'm on so many meds I can't sustain the focus. Besides, I never really loved to write. Not the way so many other writers seem to. It's a hard, lonely struggle. But I'm not telling you anything you don't already know. You've had struggles yourself."

"That I have."

"Happily, I was fortunate enough to be well paid for it, so I'm set for life. And I intend to spend as much free time as I can with Lola until and unless she turns out to be a professional con artist who's out to burn me."

"For your sake, I hope the lieutenant's background check doesn't turn anything up."

Groat managed a faint smile. "Thank you. And, Lieutenant, I'm sorry about what's going on with Norma. She's the best editor I've ever had."

The beeper on Very's belt came to life. He was being paged.

"May I use your phone?" he asked Groat.

"Of course. There's one in the kitchen."

Very got up, went in there, and phoned in. He wasn't on the phone for very long, and I couldn't make out what he was saying, but when he returned, he had a stunned look on his face and was moving unusually slowly, one foot in front of the other. "We've got to go," he said to me woodenly. "There's been an incident on the downtown 1 train in Times Square. It was . . . it was the train that Norma and Alissa were riding home on together. I had two plainclothesmen riding in the same car with them just to play it safe. I begged her to go home in a patrol car but she refused. Stubborn. So goddamned stubborn . . ."

I studied him with great concern. "Lieutenant, is everything okay?"

"No, dude. Everything's not okay."

CHAPTER SIX

We couldn't get anywhere near Times Square. It was gridlock city.

Very pounded the steering wheel and let out a roar of exasperation before he double-parked halfway up the block on Broadway, jumped out, and started running toward the subway station. Lulu and I took off after him. He still wasn't back to full speed from his gunshot wound. I could tell because he was running as fast as he could and we had no trouble catching up to him and staying right with him.

The stairways to the subway station at Forty-Second Street were surrounded by at least a dozen blue-and-whites, several unmarked Crown Vics, and a pair of EMT vans. Very flashed his shield at a beefy patrolman who was blocking one of the entrances. He stepped aside and we tore our way downstairs, jumped the turnstile—Lulu went under it—and made a beeline for the stairway to the downtown 1, 2, and 3 trains. Again, a beefy patrolman blocked our way. Again, Very flashed his shield and he let us through. What we found when got to the platform was total mayhem—an unruly rush hour mob of people who wanted to get home but couldn't.

They'd been ordered to stay put because they were potential witnesses to a crime.

The downtown 1 train sat there with its doors closed, crammed with yammering, outraged passengers who had to remain on board, whether they'd intended to get off at Times Square or not. The 2 train had been halted in the tunnel just before it reached the tracks across the platform, so anyone who was waiting for it had a long wait, as did the passengers who were on that 2 train trapped in the tunnel with no idea when they'd see daylight again.

The only passengers who'd been allowed to get off the 1 train were those who'd been riding in the third car from the rear. They'd been herded to a corner of the platform and were giving a half-dozen patrolmen their witness statements and contact information.

These passengers didn't look outraged. They looked horrified.

As we elbowed our way closer to the train, I saw why—a body lay under a tarp on the floor near the middle door of that third car from the rear. Transit cops were stationed on the platform there to keep people away, and two EMTs were keeping a close watch over it while they waited for the ME to arrive.

Two other EMTs were at the rear of the car, bandaging Norma's right forearm. She had a blanket wrapped around her shoulders and was sobbing. Two plainclothesmen were seated across the car from her with stricken expressions on their faces. Very went charging down the car toward her. When she caught sight of him, she let out a pained cry and held out her arm to him. He fell onto the seat beside her and hugged her and kissed her and kissed her some more.

"Oh God, you had me so scared!" he gasped, his chest heaving from his mad dash to get to her. "They paged me and I was so afraid it was *you*!"

"It was *supposed* to be me, not Alissa," she sobbed. "I *know* it was. Poor Alissa . . ."

"Are you okay?"

"It was awful. But I—I'm okay."

"*Is* she?" he asked one of the EMTs who was working on her forearm.

"She was a bit shocky when we got here, Lieutenant. But her vitals are normal now. She's aware and alert. Got scraped up pretty good but didn't complain of pain when I applied pressure to her wrist and arm. No broken bones. These floors are germ central, so we've cleaned and disinfected the wound thoroughly and now we'll bandage it. If she starts experiencing any kind of throbbing pain tonight, take her to the emergency room, but I think she'll be okay—unlike her friend over there," he added, glancing over his shoulder at the body under the tarp.

Very got up and started down the car toward it. I sat down with Norma and gave her a hug while Lulu climbed into her lap and licked her face.

"How are you doing, Coach?" I asked gently, as the EMT crew finished bandaging her up.

"Hoagy, I'm the one who's supposed to be dead under that tarp," she moaned. "He was coming after *me* with that knife, not Alissa. Why would anyone want to kill Alissa? God, do her parents know?"

"I'm sure they'll be informed."

Very spoke for a moment to the EMTs who were standing next to the tarp. He knelt and raised a corner of it high enough so that he could see what he needed to see of Alissa's body, then lowered it and started back toward us, his jaw working furiously on a fresh piece of bubble gum. He faced the two plainclothesmen who were seated across from Norma, hands on his hips. Both were young guys, one white, the other Black. Both were dressed like construction workers in heavy flannel shirts and jeans. Both looked extremely downcast. Very didn't say anything to them. Not yet. Just shook his head in disbelief before he turned back to Norma.

The EMTs were packing up. "She's good to go, Lieutenant," one of them said. "But I'd let her sit here for a few more minutes, and she should take it easy this evening. Wash and bandage her arm again tomorrow." And off they went.

Very knelt before her. "Tell me what happened."

Norma gazed down at him, shoving her horn-rimmed glasses up her nose. "I don't *know* what happened. We left the office together, walked over to Broadway and West Fiftieth, and caught the 1 train for Christopher Street just like we usually do. Chattered about this and that. Don't ask me what, because I d-don't . . ." She trailed off, starting to cry again.

Very patted her knee reassuringly. "It's okay. Don't worry about it. So you caught the train, pulled in here at Times Square station, and . . . ?"

She sniffled. "The car was crowded. We were both standing."

"Where?"

"Over there in the middle of the car, clutching on to the same pole. We were right next to each other. When the train pulled into the station, it slowed up and stopped. People started squeezing their way past us to get to the door. I could see that the platform was crowded and it was going to be a real sardine fest of people trying to get on while the other people were trying to get off. Rush hour at Times Square. So what else is new?" She paused, frowning. "Except then something weird happened . . ."

"Weird, as in . . .?"

"First, the doors didn't open, and then the train started backing up before it stopped again with a—a lurch."

"What kind of a lurch?"

"Lieutenant, I just talked to a guy from the MTA," the Black plainclothesman interjected. "He said the train operator overshot the end of the platform by about a foot. The brakes on these old trains suck. They've had new trains on order for two years. For now, they do the best they can, which means the operator had to put it in reverse, inch his way back a foot, and then hit the brakes again—not very smoothly. The passengers were already up out of their seats, crowding toward the doors . . ."

"Right," Norma said, nodding her head. "So everyone got jostled and thrown around."

"The guy from the MTA also mentioned that the operator was finishing up the end of a long shift," the plainclothesman added. "He'll be put on leave while an investigation is conducted, considering the circumstances."

"Talk to me about the circumstances," Very said to Norma. "What happened?"

"Someone who was shoving his way toward the door lost his balance while the train was backing up, knocked me to the floor, and suddenly I—I heard Alissa let out this horrible gasp of pain." Norma's voice quavered, her eyes filling with tears. "Then this guy fought his way through the crowd, ran out the door as it opened, and took off. That's when I realized Alissa was slumping to the floor and that she was . . . she was *gone*. She died so fast she didn't have a chance to say a word. One minute she was there, the next minute she wasn't."

"He must have stabbed her right through the heart," Very said grimly. "I've seen it happen. What did he look like?"

"He was gone so fast I barely saw him. He wasn't tall, kind of stocky. It was supposed to be *me*. He meant to kill *me*. Oh God, poor Alissa!"

Very patted her on the knee. "You relax with Hoagy and Lulu for another minute, okay?" He stood back up and returned to Norma's security detail. "Okay, tell it."

"Loo, nothing like this has ever happened to me before," the white cop said hoarsely. "I feel like shit."

"It happens. Part of the job," Very said impatiently. "Tell it."

"We were on them," the Black cop said. "Staying as close to them as possible. But you know how it is. There's a crush when the train pulls in. People pushing, shoving. And then the operator messed up and the train went thumpety-bump and people got thrown around before the door opened. The perp didn't tip his hand at all. Just seemed to be trying to get off, same as everyone else—until he flew at the two of them. Except he got jostled, knocked Miss Fives to the floor like she said, and stuck the other one. I didn't get a look at the knife, but whatever he was carrying, it was plenty sharp, because her friend was history within seconds. And so was he. Fought his way out the door, low to the ground, throwing elbows, and went sprinting across the platform. I fought my way through the crowd, yelling 'Police!' and went running up the stairs after him, but by then he'd reached the station level, and you know this place. There are a million different directions to go—the stairs to the street, the stairs to the uptown trains, the passageway to the shuttle to Grand Central. This place is an underground maze. I don't know where he went. All I know is he was gone."

"And that he blew it," Very said. "Didn't kill his intended victim."

I said, "How can you be absolutely sure that his intended victim *wasn't* Alissa, Lieutenant?"

Very stared at me a moment before he said, "You're right. I can't be absolutely sure about anything yet." He turned back to Norma's security detail. "What was he wearing?"

"A brown rain jacket made out of nylon, maybe," the white cop answered. "Under that, a gray hooded sweatshirt with the hood up. A dark blue wool stocking cap and wraparound sunglasses. That says pro to me. I mean, you couldn't make out a single distinguishing feature if you tried."

"Anything else?"

"Work gloves. Baggy jeans, work boots. Stocky, like Miss Fives said. Maybe five-eight."

"I feel like shit about this, too," the Black cop said, his voice cracking with emotion.

"Don't blame yourselves. Either of you. We can't stop them every single time no matter how hard we try. Got it?"

They ducked their heads, nodding.

Two balding, overweight men got on at the other end of the car and made their way toward Alissa's body under the tarp. Both wore raincoats and carried black satchels.

I recognized them from previous encounters of the worst kind as the medical examiner and his assistant. They were followed by two younger, slimmer guys who were wearing FORENSICS windbreakers and carrying satchels of their own.

"You two stay put and keep an eye on Norma," Very said to the plainclothesmen.

"Right, Loo," they responded.

Lulu stayed put, too, her head in Norma's lap as Norma stroked her gently.

I joined Very. We stood there watching them lift the tarp. Both wore latex gloves. Alissa was lying with her cheek against the floor, eyes open, her face a ghostly white. She'd lost a shoe somewhere. Had died with her toenails painted blue. There was not a lot of blood on the floor. Surprisingly little, actually. The ME and his assistant stepped aside and patiently allowed the forensics duo, who also wore latex gloves, to unbutton Alissa's raincoat and remove it. They bagged and tagged it to examine later at the lab. Not that they'd find anything, if you're asking me, but it was possible that a unique, traceable fiber had transferred from her killer's nylon jacket to her coat. That does happen—in bad TV cop shows.

The ME knelt with a grunt, the better to get a look at the knife's entry wound in Alissa's burgundy silk turtleneck. It was in the left side of her back at around the bra line. "I saw someone cut like this in Brownsville a few months ago, Lieutenant," he said. "Gang killing. Killer used a pointed razor-sharp, double-edged switchblade."

"I hate those damned things."

"I'm not too fond of them myself. And you can buy one at any knife shop in the five boroughs. Hide it up your sleeve and with a flick it's open. The double-edged blade is four inches long. Plenty long enough to do what it did to a slender young girl like this one."

"Which is what?" Very asked him.

"I'll have to get her on my table to confirm it, but my guess is that it penetrated between her ribs directly into her heart and severed the lower half of her left ventricle. She would have been unconscious in seconds and bled out internally in less than two minutes, which is why we're not looking at a pool of blood on the floor here. The EMTs couldn't have saved her. She had no chance."

"How strong a killer are we talking about?"

"He wouldn't have to be strong at all. The knife did all the work for him."

Lulu joined us now, nudging my leg with her head. I reached down and patted her. "Any chance a woman could have done it?" I asked.

The ME shot a curious look at Very, who nodded at him to go ahead and answer me.

"No reason a good-sized woman couldn't have done it," he replied. "Especially if she had the benefit of a shove that threw her into the victim." He turned to his assistant. "Let's get her bagged up and out of here."

His assistant unzipped a black body bag and they got ready to load her into it. A pair of big strong cops in uniform were standing outside of the door waiting to carry her up to the ME's van.

"Any idea where she was standing?" one of the forensics investigators asked Very.

"She had a grip on this pole right here."

"Okay, good. We'll want to dust that."

"Her killer was wearing work gloves," Very pointed out. "You won't get any prints."

"But we still gotta do what we gotta do. Know what I'm saying, Loo?"

Very nodded. "Right," he said heavily.

"You okay, Loo?" the other forensics investigator asked.

"Been better." Very turned and glanced down the car at Norma.

I looked at him looking at Norma, pretty sure he was thinking about that second death threat:

Your boyfriend can't save you. No one can.

The forensics duo got busy dusting the pole for prints. Lulu found Alissa's missing shoe twenty feet away under a seat and let out a bark.

That, too, got bagged and tagged.

Then we started back toward Norma and her security detail.

Very's jaw was still working his bubble gum. "You don't really think she was murdered by a woman, do you?" he asked me.

"I think you shouldn't rule it out, that's all."

"I'm not ruling anything out. But first I have to deal with the entire New York City press corps, which is waiting for me outside the stairs on Forty-Second Street. Then I have to get Norma snugged in at home."

"She'll have zero security in that place of hers."

"She'll have me. And a patrol car will be parked outside all night."

"I have to make a phone call, okay? I'll catch up with you in a second." I went out the open door and started across the platform. Lulu joined me. There was trouble in the air, so she wasn't letting me go anywhere by myself. By now the police had let the other passengers and people waiting on the platform take off. It was eerily deserted. No one was waiting for the next 1 train. No one was waiting across the platform for the 2 or 3. The 2 that had been halted in the tunnel had pulled in and let its passengers off. The train sat there empty. Both tunnels were shut down for now. I went up the stairs to the yellow security tape, where a cop in uniform was stationed, and told him that Lulu and I were associates of Lieutenant Very and would be right back. He looked at us curiously but shrugged his shoulders and let us through. We started our way through the crowded station. People seemed to be rushing in six different directions at once. There were stairways that went up, stairways that went down. It was a maze of passageways, just like the plainclothesman had said, one of which led toward the shuttle to Grand Central. I steered us in that direction, Lulu staying close to me. There were stalls near the shuttle that sold newspapers and such things as candy corn, cold drinks, and empanadas. I found a pay phone there and called Merilee.

"Hi, darling," she said to me when she picked up.

"Hi, back at you."

"Your voice sounds funny. And I can barely hear you. What's going on?"

"I'm in the Times Square subway station, for one thing."

"And . . .?"

"And someone just tried to kill Norma on the 1 train."

She let out a gasp. "Is she okay?"

"A bit scraped up and scared as hell. But her editorial assistant, Alissa, is dead. Stabbed right through the heart."

Merilee fell silent for a moment. "These crazy death threats she's been getting aren't so funny anymore, are they?" Her voice choked with emotion. "Not that they ever were."

"Listen, Norma lives in a studio walk-up on Bank Street. Would it be okay if . . ."

"Tell Norma and Very that I insist they spend the night here. We have plenty of spare rooms. A secure lobby with twenty-four-hour doormen and sofas where he can station more men if he wants to."

"I was hoping you'd say that. That's what I was going to ask."

"As if you had to ask."

"I'll extend the invite."

"It's not an invite. It's an order. If Very gives you any guff, tell him to call me and I'll read him the riot act."

"Something tells me I won't encounter any guff. He's pretty shook up himself."

"Darling, how are you and Lulu?"

"We're okay. She's standing right here by my side on high alert, making absolutely sure nothing happens to me. It's just been a long, hard day. Very and I spoke to three different authors whom Norma had recently let go, which meant listening to hours and hours of crazy talk from crazy people. And now this has happened." I let out a sigh. "Have I told you recently that I love you, blond person?"

"You've never told me that. Not once in all the years I've known you."

"Liar mouth."

"I love you back, tall guy. Get home as soon as you can. I'll make up one of the spare bedrooms and put out fresh towels and soap in the bathroom."

"We'll have to swing by Norma's place to fetch them some clean clothes. Don't bother with dinner. I'll get us a couple of pizzas later."

The cop at the top of the stairs made good on his shrug and let us back in. We made our way across the platform to Norma's train.

Very was seated next to her with his arm around her. "What took you so long, dude?"

"I've been making arrangements."

"What kind?"

"You're moving in with us tonight. We live in a high-security building with twenty-four-hour doormen and a huge lobby where you can station your security detail. You'll have a choice of two guest bedrooms and your own bath. Don't even think about saying no or you'll have to fight it out with Merilee, and I guarantee you you'll lose. Besides, Norma has work to do."

She frowned at me. "Work? What work?"

"You have to read my first chapter tonight. I went over your edits this morning. I'm on a tight deadline, as you may recall."

Norma looked at Very hopefully. I could tell she loved the idea and he hated it. He didn't like to accept help from anyone. Wasn't his style. "It's awfully nice of Merilee," she said to him.

"Real generous," he grunted. "But not necessary."

I shook my head at him. "Don't you want Norma to feel safe and comfortable?"

"Yeah, of course."

"So let's drive your bucket of bolts down to her place, collect whatever you'll need, and head uptown, okay?"

"Okay . . ." he said reluctantly. "But first we have to fight our way through the media to get out of here," he said as we started our way across the platform toward the stairs, Norma's two-man security detail staying with us.

"How much will you tell them?"

"Inspector Feldman taught me years ago that if you don't know anything—which, hello, I don't—to give a brief statement, say you have no time to answer questions right now, and then just barrel your way through them."

When we climbed the stairs to Forty-Second Street, we found ourselves surrounded by an army of news cameramen, newspaper photographers, and reporters. The lights from all the cameras were practically blinding.

"WHAT CAN YOU TELL US, LIEUTENANT?" a half-dozen reporters shouted at once as I shielded Norma behind me.

Very stood at the top of the steps, collecting his thoughts as Norma's two plainclothesmen flanked him. "I'm going to tell you this only once, so pay attention," he said in a loud, clear voice. "There was a stabbing incident at approximately five forty-five P.M. on the downtown 1 train in Times Square station. We have one fatality. I'm not prepared to identify the victim until the next of kin have been notified. The suspect is at large, identity and motive unknown. We've taken statements from eyewitnesses. I have no further details at this time. If you want to know when normal train service will be restored, you'll have to talk to the MTA. That's all I have to say." When they immediately started shouting more questions, he said, "I've got no time for follow-ups. I'm working the case." Then he pushed his way through them and hurried toward his cruiser, limping slightly. That mad dash from his car to the scene of the stabbing had definitely given his recovering leg wound some trouble. Norma, Lulu, and I stayed right with him. The media horde started to follow us, shouting more questions. The two plainclothesmen blocked their path and ordered them to back off.

When we reached his Crown Vic, he unlocked it and climbed in, wincing slightly. Lulu claimed her spot next to him in the front seat. I joined them up there. Norma rode in back.

"You doing okay, Baby Girl?" he asked her.

"Yeah, don't worry about me. But what about you?"

"What a*bout* me?"

"You're limping, Romeo."

"It's nothing. Just overworked it," he grumbled as he backed the Crown Vic up a hundred yards to West Forty-Third, made a right, and tore out of there. I was beginning to feel every single pothole in my lower back by the time he made a left onto Ninth Avenue and shot his way downtown toward the West Village.

"You handled that like a real pro, Lieutenant. You told them everything and nothing in less than sixty seconds."

"Dude?"

"Yes, Lieutenant?"

"I *am* a real pro."

"Of course you are. That was what we in the publishing world call a literary allusion. Right, Norma?"

She didn't respond. Wasn't listening to us. She just stared out her window, lost in grief.

The two-way radio on his dash squawked. He reached for it and said, "Very. Go."

What followed was a back-and-forth combination of static, numerical mumbo jumbo, and cop-talk gibberish. I understood only about 10 percent of it, although I did make out the name Feldman. Somehow—don't ask me how—Very seemed to understand every word Feldman said, and vice versa. They must send them to a special school for that. After the chief of detectives barked "Feldman OUT!" Very clipped the radio back on the dash as we continued our non-smooth ride downtown. I would swear he purposely went out of his way to hit every pothole dead center.

"What was that all about?" I asked him as my lower back went into spasms.

"Feldman has notified Alissa's parents in Westchester. They're totally devastated but will come into the city in the morning to formally identify her body. He's sending a man out to pick them up."

"That's very considerate."

"Standard procedure."

"What else?"

"He wants to know who the bastard in the hoodie is and how in the hell he got away."

"Oh, is that all?"

"I told him I'd run it for him in detail as soon as I get Norma settled in, which was the best I could come up with considering I have no idea who the bastard in the hoodie is or how in the hell he got away."

"Quick thinking."

"Hey, I'm just trying to keep my head above water. He also wanted to know if my 'emotional involvement' would be a problem. I assured him it wouldn't be. But I guarantee you he'll yank me if I don't get results right away."

"You will. I have complete confidence in you."

Lulu let out a low whoop on the seat between us.

"And I'm not the only one who does."

I'd never been to Norma's place before. She lived in a quaint, well-tended brownstone on a quaint, well-tended section of Bank Street. Two patrol cars were parked out front, keeping an eye on the place. Very gave them a thumbs-up as we started inside. Norma had a tiny studio apartment on the second floor that bore a striking resemblance to her office, what with the books and manuscripts that were piled everywhere. The only difference was that there was a bed and a Pullman kitchen with a miniature table for two. A couple of doors led to what I assumed were a bathroom and a closet. I don't usually feel claustrophobic but with the three of us, Lulu, and Lulu's breath crowded in there, I did.

"We'll make it quick," Very said. "Grab a beer if you want one."

"I'm good, thanks."

"Jeez, Baby Girl, you've got sixteen messages on your phone machine," Very said, glancing at it. "Probably reporters calling you for a statement."

"I don't want to talk to anyone," she said, her voice rising with emotion. The phone proceeded to ring once again. "Let the machine take it."

After the beep, the voice of a woman from the *New York Times* invaded the small apartment. "Hello, Ms. Fives. I'm sorry for your loss but I was hoping to get a statement from you about your assistant, Alissa Loeb, for tomorrow's paper."

"Take the call," Very said to her sharply. "Pick it up."

"Why?" Norma demanded.

"Because you'll keep getting pestered by the entire press corps if you don't—including the thugs from the *New York Post*—who'll start nosing around and won't stop until they find out about the death threats. It's the *Times*," he said as the woman continued to drone into the machine, leaving several different phone numbers where she could be reached. "You give her a quote and the other papers will just lift it. Say it once and be done with it. Hurry, before she hangs up."

"But I—I don't know what to say."

"Not to worry." I reached for the notepad and pen on her kitchen table and started scribbling.

Very grabbed for the phone. "Hello? Yeah, yeah, she's here. Just walked in the door. Who, me? I live across the hall. Yeah, I'm sure she'll want to give you a statement. Hang on a sec . . ."

I tore the piece of paper from the notepad and handed it to her.

She scanned it, nodding her head, took the phone from Very, and said, "Hello? Yes, this is Norma Fives. Alissa Loeb was an outstanding employee with a promising future in publishing. She was also a dear friend. I'll miss her terribly. I'm totally devastated and I have nothing more to say right now, okay? Thank you."

Very motioned for her to hang up. She hung up, letting out a sigh of relief.

"Good work, Coach."

Then the two of them got busy throwing some clothes and toiletry items in overnight bags.

"Oh, hey, dude?" Very said as he carried his bag to the front door and dropped it there. Norma was still packing.

"Yes, Lieutenant?"

He lowered his voice. "Thanks for the invite. She'll feel a lot more secure at your place than here."

"Merilee's the one who you should thank. It was her idea."

"Yeah, but it was you who called her. So thanks. And, not to worry, we'll be gone in a day, two tops."

"What's going to happen in a day, two tops?"

"I'm going to crack this case."

"You sound pretty sure of yourself for a guy who limps around like Chester on *Gunsmoke*."

"Do not."

"Do."

"Do not."

"Do."

"My leg just gets tired at the end of a long day, that's all."

"If you say so."

"I say so. And I am."

"Am what?"

"Going to crack this case. You can put it in the bank, dude. No one tries to kill the love of my life and gets away with it. Nobody."

CHAPTER SEVEN

There was a blue-and-white parked outside of our building with a man in uniform behind the wheel. Another man in uniform was stationed in the lobby along with our two doormen. One of the doormen, Tony, told me that the Mets were trailing two-zip in the third. Damned weather.

We rode the elevator up to the sixteenth floor in grim silence, Very and Norma each toting an overnight bag. I carried her book bag for her since she admitted that her bandaged arm was starting to feel sore. Merilee, who was dressed in an old flannel shirt and jeans, gave Norma a big hug, Norma's bony nose almost disappearing in Merilee's belly button. There were times, especially around Merilee, when Norma seemed as if she were still not fully grown.

"Merilee, it's so nice of you to do this," she said, her voice choking with emotion.

"Nonsense. We're friends. Friends look out for each other, didn't you know that? I've made up the bed in the bigger of our spare rooms because it has more closet space." Merilee led our guests in the direction of the hallway. "Your bathroom is across the hall. I'm afraid the only spare room with an attached bath has been converted into a certain author's office. I've put some fresh soap and towels out. If you need a toothbrush or anything, don't hesitate to holler."

Lulu headed straight for the kitchen for an anchovy. I got her one, and put down some 9Lives mackerel for her, too, in case she wanted her dinner. Then I rejoined our guests.

"This bedroom is bigger than my whole apartment," Norma was saying, gazing around in awe at the queen-sized bed with its antique quilt and freshly ironed pillowcases. Merilee abhors wrinkled pillowcases and had made sure to press them before Norma and Very arrived. "Do you have a maid?"

Merilee let out a hoot. "As if. We're just regular folks here."

"Then you'll have to teach me how to make a bed sometime. Romeo is always teasing me that none of my corners are straight."

"It'll be my pleasure. Every Miss Porter's girl knows how to make a bed properly. I imagine you'd like to unpack. What would you like to do after that? Eat, drink?"

"I'd like to stretch out for a few minutes, if you don't mind," Norma said wearily.

"Yeah, why don't you do that?" Very urged her. "You've been through a lot."

In fact, she skipped the unpacking part entirely. Just kicked off her shoes and stretched out on the bed, totally drained. Merilee grabbed a spare blanket from the closet and put it over her.

Norma snuggled in gratefully. "I should call my parents and let them know I'm okay, but I really don't feel like talking to anyone right now."

"I'll call them," Very offered.

"You'd do that for me?"

"Not a problem. I'll tell them you would have called them yourself but that you were given a sedative. And I'll assure them that you're in safe hands."

"Which you are," Merilee said.

Lulu climbed up onto the bed and stretched out with her, her head on Norma's tummy.

"Lulu's just the sweetest," Norma said. "It's almost as if she can read my emotions."

"Trust me, she can," I said. "We'll let you relax for a while. Just let us know when you get hungry."

"Not so fast, writer boy. You said the chapter one edits are ready for me to look at."

"Rats, I was hoping you'd forgotten about that."

"Not a chance."

"Ordinarily, I'd prefer to go over it one more time before giving it back to you. But if you really want to have a look, I'll fetch it for you."

"Please do. I'm desperate to keep my mind occupied. And I'll need a sharpened red pencil."

I fetched the chapter and a sharpened red pencil for her from my office. She took them from me as I flicked on the nightstand lamp, her eyes eager with anticipation as she immediately went to work.

"Oh, good," she said happily. "I was afraid you were going to fight me about your opening sentence."

"Nope, you were a hundred percent right. I must have rewritten it six times, was never happy with it, and you knew the reason why."

She focused her full attention on the manuscript now, barely aware that we were still in the room. Her power of concentration was enviable. We left her there with Lulu dozing on her hip.

"Dude, would it be okay if I use the phone in your office to call her parents?" Very asked. "I also promised Feldman I'd call him back."

"Help yourself."

"Thanks." He went down to the end of the hall, still limping slightly, and closed the door behind him.

Merilee and I stood there together in the hall for a moment before I said, "This is weird. It's almost as if I woke up from a conk on the head and we suddenly have two kids."

She narrowed her green eyes at me. "Are you getting any ideas, handsome?"

"Don't go there."

"Just checking. You don't mention children very often. In fact, never."

"Yeah, well, there's a reason for that."

I went in our bedroom, took off the blazer, slacks, shirt, and tie I'd been wearing all day, and changed into my torn jeans, my favorite old navy-blue turtleneck sweater, and ancient black Chuck Taylor All Star high-tops.

I stopped off in the kitchen to pour a glass of Côtes du Rhône and open two bottles of Bass Ale before I joined Merilee in the living room, where she was seated in an armchair gazing out at the park.

"Thank you, darling," she said when I handed her the glass of wine.

I set one of the Bass Ales on the coffee table and took a long drink from the other before I turned down the lights so we could enjoy a better look at the sky clearing over the park. Then I flopped down on the sofa and took another long drink.

"Was it awful?" Merilee asked me.

"Certainly my idea of awful. Alissa was stabbed through the heart with a double-edged switchblade simply because she happened to be riding home with Norma and the brakes on those old subway trains are ready for the scrap heap. Norma feels responsible for her death. Hell, she *is* responsible for her death. That's not going to be easy for her to deal with."

"I can't believe the killer got away."

"It happened in a flash, apparently. And you know the Times Square station. It's an incredibly easy place to disappear."

She sipped her wine thoughtfully. "I have to confess that I didn't believe it was for real. I thought it was just a disgruntled author behaving badly the same way disgruntled actors behave badly. People like us, we make a lot of noise, but we don't actually *do* anything."

"Believe me, I felt the same way. And when Boyd Samuels took that dive off his terrace, I thought, well, this is a guy who's been screwed up for years, but when it came time to *do* something, he took his despair out on himself, not Norma."

She nodded. "I know two actors who've committed suicide. Two more who died from what were called 'accidental overdoses.' "

Very was on the phone for a good long while before I heard his footsteps in the hall and he joined us, hobbling slightly.

"There's a Bass Ale in here with your name on it," I said to him.

"The answer to my prayers." He found it there on the coffee table and took a long drink, sighing gratefully.

"Your leg's really bothering you, isn't it?"

He grimaced. "Nah. It's fine."

"Beg to differ. When we were sprinting to the murder scene from your car, I could have sped past you if I'd wanted to."

"Like hell you could have."

"Lieutenant, you're forgetting that in addition to being the third-best spear chucker in the entire Ivy League, I was also first alternate on our mile relay team. Can I get you a couple of Tylenol?"

He sat down on the sofa, puffing out his cheeks. "Wouldn't say no."

I got the bottle from the powder room and tossed it to him. He helped himself to two and washed them down with a swig of his Bass. "Thanks, dude."

The three of us drank in silence for a moment before I asked him, "What did Inspector Feldman have to say?"

"He was obsessed with the big picture."

"Which big picture would that be?"

"The one about the millions of exhausted straphangers who get home from work, plop down on the sofa with a cold one, turn on the news with Chuck Scarborough and Sue Simmons, and get smacked in the face with *this*—an attractive young editorial assistant at a major publishing house getting stabbed to death on a subway train in Midtown Manhattan by some nut who then disappeared into thin air. It summons up memories of David Berkowitz and Bernie Goetz. Scares the crap out of them. We need them to feel calm, or at least that's what the mayor told Feldman either five, six, or seven times. Feldman said he lost count. The mayor also reminded him that it's bad for the city's image as a tourist destination. The people in Akron, Ohio, will decide that New York is too dangerous and go to Disney World instead, because nobody ever gets stabbed to death in Orlando. They just get eaten by alligators."

"Does that really happen or are you just on a rant?"

Very didn't bother to answer me. "Feldman also brought up my involvement with Norma again. Floated having someone else take over the case. I said no way, Jose."

"You actually called him Jose?"

Very smiled faintly. "Okay, no. That part was a lie. Damn, I can't put anything past you, can I, dude?"

"Don't even try, Romeo."

"Meanwhile, he's got a major task force working every possible angle as we speak."

"Are you going public with Norma's death threats?"

"Not yet. We're hoping to catch the bastard before it comes to that. Once we mention the death threats, you just know it'll pull in the Boyd Samuels suicide. Someone at HWA is bound to spill that Norma got him fired. And then all sorts of stories about how ugly the publishing industry is will start to spread—which is one more thing the city doesn't need."

"Neither does Norma," Merilee said quietly.

"Neither does Norma," he agreed, starting to nod his head to his own rock 'n' roll beat. "Something like this would put a stain on her career. People won't forget."

"That's one thing you can count on. People never forget." I gazed at Merilee. "What about you?"

"What about me, Mister?"

"How was your day?"

"Well, I ironed some pillowcases."

"Aside from that."

"I read two original screenplays that I've been offered."

"Did you like either of them?"

She shook her head of golden hair. "You would be amazed at the poor quality of the writing."

"Actually, no, I wouldn't."

She let out a soft laugh. "Darling, why is it that so many of these young screenwriters only know how to write artificial movie characters, not real people who have genuine emotions?"

"Because their entire life experience consists of growing up in the suburbs and then going to film school, where they pass their time sitting in a dark room staring at moving images on a wall. They've never been out in the world and talked to real people. Never traveled. They have no other writing experience, either. Haven't been journalists, novelists, playwrights . . . Which reminds me, I still think you should do a Broadway revival of *Cat on a Hot Tin Roof*."

"I've been thinking about getting back on stage, I must admit. There's nothing quite as exhilarating, and terrifying, as putting yourself out there in front of a live audience. But I'm too old to play Maggie the cat."

"Trust me, you're not."

She beamed at me. "Flatterer."

I finished my beer and turned to Very. "Want to stroll over to Columbus with me and pick up a couple of pizzas, or do you need to rest that leg?"

"Nah, I'll join you. It'll do me good, as long as we don't walk too fast."

"I think you can count on that," I said as I climbed slowly to my feet, my back getting tighter by the minute.

"I'll make us a salad," Merilee said. "I might even set the table."

I bent down and kissed her on the cheek. "Thank you."

Then I put on my flight jacket and Very and I headed for the door. Lulu was still sacked out with Norma. The elevator deposited us in the lobby, where Tony the doorman had two uniformed patrolmen for company. He informed me that my Mets were now trailing the Phillies 5–0 thanks to a three-run Darren Daulton dinger.

The evening was cool but comfortable. We strolled slowly toward Columbus Avenue on West Seventy-Seventh, walking in silence for a bit and enjoying the quiet, or what passes for quiet in the city.

"Where are we headed?" Very finally asked.

"Sal's. It's a tiny neighborhood take-out place on Columbus that's been there forever. No tables. No phoning ahead. Sal is strictly old school. And he makes awesome pies."

Sal was serving a slice to a hungry businessman when we got there. His creased face lit up when he saw me. "Mr. Hoagy, it's been too long."

"It has, Sal. You're absolutely right."

"But where's Lulu?" His face fell. "She's not . . .?"

"She's totally fine. Home comforting a friend."

"Ah, good," he said with a sigh of relief.

Merilee's pizza of choice was always spinach and mushroom, so I ordered us a large one of those—with the addition of anchovies on one-quarter of it for you-know-who. After conferring with Very, I ordered a second large pie topped with sausage and peppers. While Sal got busy making them, Very and I bought a six-pack of Bass from the corner grocery and sat on the curb out front of Sal's to wait. I opened two bottles with my Swiss Army knife and handed Very one. We drank deeply. Then I dug my Chesterfields out of my jacket pocket, tapped the pack, pulled one out, and lit it with Grandfather's Varaflame lighter, dragging on it deeply.

Very peered at me. "Since when do you smoke?"

"Used to smoke two packs a day before I quit. But while I was writing my novel, I allowed myself one cigarette every evening as an after-dinner treat. For some reason, I felt like having one now."

"Dude?"

"What is it, Lieutenant?"

"Can I have one, too?"

I handed him the pack and lit his cigarette for him.

He dragged on it as deeply as I had. "I used to smoke two packs a day myself. Still get a craving when things get crazy," he said as we sat there on the curb, smoking and drinking. "I love that girl. If I'd lost her . . . damn, I don't even want to think to think about it."

"So don't. Keep your mind busy working the case. What has Feldman's task force picked up so far?"

"They ran a check on Richard Groat's call girl honey, Lola Lux, née Jean Donkin. She's twenty-eight and actually is from Winnipeg. Has been living in New York since she was twenty-one. She was questioned four years ago while she was working for an escort service. No charges were filed. This was back before she went to work for the high-end madam that Groat's lawyer buddy set him up with. But hang on, because there's an interesting twist in the road up ahead. While she was working for the escort service, she lived with a mobbed-up hit man named Nicholas Dipoto, better known as Slick Nick."

I stubbed out my cigarette. "Hmm, this sounds promising."

"You'd think so, except Slick Nick disappeared three years ago."

"Disappeared, as in . . ."

"No one has seen or heard from him, meaning either he cleared out of town or he's at the bottom of the East River. I'd put my money on the latter. He was a person of interest in the shooting of a loan shark at the time. Lola was questioned about his disappearance but claimed to have no knowledge of his whereabouts. She now lives alone in a studio apartment in a high-rise on First Avenue. There's a possibility that she's mixed up in this. She must be acquainted with some of Slick Nick's old running buddies. And, who knows, maybe she genuinely loves Groat and would do anything he asked her to if it would make him happy. Mind if I have another cigarette?"

"Help yourself." I lit another one for myself, too. Also opened two more bottles of Bass. By the time the pies were ready, we'd need to buy another six-pack to take home with us. "Great minds work alike, Lieutenant. Or at least *our* minds work alike. I keep circling directly back to Groat. We're talking about a guy who's been plotting clever heists for half of his adult life. I can definitely see him coming up with the idea of sending Norma those old-school death threats. And who's to say he wasn't genuinely pissed off when she lowered the boom on him? Who's to say he didn't convince Lola to help him get even with Norma by hiring one of Slick Nick's old running buddies to knife her on that subway train?"

Very mulled it over. "It certainly plays. I'm going to bring her in for a guided tour of an interrogation room tomorrow morning and see what shakes out."

"Sounds like a plan," I said as a blue-and-white pulled up at the curb next to us.

A patrolman rolled down his window and said, "This isn't a saloon, gentlemen."

Very flashed his shield.

The patrolman's eyes widened. "Sorry, didn't recognize you, Loo. Some shitstorm at Times Square, hey?"

"Yeah. Just doing a little decompressing while we're waiting for our pizza."

"Have a good one." They drove on.

"Boy, am I glad you came with me."

"Why?"

"Because if I'd been sitting here on the curb drinking beer all by myself, I can guarantee you I would have made an obnoxious wisecrack and they'd have hauled me in for public intoxication and assaulting a police officer."

He flashed a grin at me. "You're such a smooth gee I keep forgetting you have a totally rowdy past. You feeling feisty?"

"I feel like getting even with Alissa's killer."

His face fell. "I'm right there with you, believe me."

I smoked my Chesterfield in silence for a moment before I said, "Amy."

He frowned at me. "Norma's sister? What about her?"

"When Norma got the first death threat, you asked her if anyone hated her. The first words out of her mouth were 'You mean other than my sister, Amy?' "

"Figure of speech. She wasn't being serious—or have you picked up something?"

"Nothing solid. Just a small tickle in the back of my brain. Lulu and I stopped by Scotty's for tuna melts this afternoon. Amy couldn't have been happier to wait on us and have a chat. She doesn't seem to resent that Norma has become a rising star in the publishing world. Told me she always felt sorry for the Mouse, as she calls her."

Very looked at me, startled. "Please don't ever use that nickname again."

"Not a problem. She said that when they were kids the Mou—Norma was super competitive and arrogant. Had no friends, no fun. All she did was sit in her room and read. Amy seems genuinely happy for her that she's successful but said that the two of them have no relationship. They never get together, never talk on the phone, nothing. She's seen your picture in the newspaper, by the way. Thinks you're cute."

"Does Amy have a boyfriend?"

"That's where the brain tickle comes in. His name is Manny Rojas. He drives a cab and has a wife and kids back home in Puerto Rico he sends money to. Bunks with his kid brother, Raoul, at the Lincoln projects in East Harlem."

"Raoul Rojas? I know that name from somewhere. Now I'm the one who's getting the brain tickle. Any idea what Raoul does for work?"

I shook my head. "It didn't come up."

"Hmm, keep talking . . ."

"Manny picked up a coffee while I was there. He's got a stocky build. So does Amy for that matter. She's at least five foot six and if you bumped into her, you'd bounce off."

He stubbed out his cigarette and said, "Is this the side of the street that you were working while I was getting reamed out by my captain?"

"That would be telling. Now that Alissa is in a body bag at the morgue, does your captain still think you've been wasting your time?"

"Don't know. Don't care. I report directly to Feldman now."

I sat there in silence for a moment as people walked along the sidewalk behind us, laughing, talking, enjoying life. No worries. No cares.

Very sat there watching me. "You okay, dude?"

"Not even close. In the immortal words of Bono, I'm ready for the laughing gas."

"I'm right there with you," he said glumly.

"So when are we going to talk about it?"

"Talk about what?"

"That it wasn't a botched murder attempt at all. That it was Alissa, not Norma, who was the intended target all along."

"It's certainly a possibility," Very conceded slowly. "But we've still got Norma's death threats to consider."

"Which may be just that—threats and nothing more."

"Okay, so run it for me. Who would want to kill Alissa?"

"We know she was having an affair with Professor McCord. Maybe she gave her fine, young body to him because he'd promised he'd help her find a better job. Maybe he didn't make good on his promise and pissed her off and she threatened to tell his wife, Jillian, about their affair—so he decided to shut her up. Or maybe she had a boyfriend who became enraged with jealousy when he found out she was also boinking McCord."

Very mulled it over. "Hmm . . ."

"Norma didn't approve of Alissa sleeping with one of Guilford House's married authors. The good professor, I've been assuming. Possibly there's another author whom Norma wasn't aware of. Might be worth looking into."

"What did *you* think of her?"

"I thought she was a climber. Also not what you'd call bashful."

"As in . . ."

"As in she made it plain from the moment I met her that she'd be happy to get naked with me any time, day or night, despite the fact it's no secret that I live with someone. She even slipped me her home phone number."

Very ran a thumb along his stubbly beard. "Which suggests to me we should check her phone records. I'll send someone to the office tomorrow to talk to the other editorial assistants, find out if she had a boyfriend. Also the gossip on who else besides McCord she was getting busy with. And we should get the keys to her apartment from her parents and have someone search it for anything that might point us to someone." He thumbed his stubble some more. "There's also McCord's wife, Jillian Goldenson, to consider. Maybe Jillian was fighting to save her marriage by knifing Alissa. Didn't you say you know her?"

"I said she wrote a profile of me back in my glory days."

"Think she'd talk to you if you gave her a call?"

I smiled inwardly. "She'll talk to me. I'll ask her about the state of her marriage."

"Sounds like you think she'll confide in you."

"Only because she will."

He nudged me with his shoulder. "Also sounds like she did more than just profile you."

"A smooth gee, as you call it, doesn't discuss such things."

"I'll take that as a yes."

"Take it any way you want. It's a free country—or so they keep telling us."

"What sort of person is Jillian?"

"Fearless. The magazine has sent her to Mogadishu, Kuwait, wherever the action is. She's one tough reporter. Good writer, too. McCord did tell us she was coming back from Washington today, but he didn't say what time. Do you really think she's in play?"

"I think we've got to eliminate her as a suspect."

"Agreed. I'll call her in the morning."

"MR. HOAGY!" Sal called across the sidewalk. "ALL SET HERE!"

I climbed to my feet, groaning from the stiffness in my lower back courtesy of Very's Crown Vic, paid Sal for the pies, thanked him profusely, and waited outside the corner grocery store, inhaling the pies' fragrant aromas while Very went inside to buy another six-pack of Bass. He'd opened the last two bottles of the first six-pack and left the empties inside. Then he handed me mine and we strolled back to the apartment, sipping them, which would mean we'd each had four beers before dinner. But it had been that kind of a day. I still wasn't feeling even remotely relaxed.

By the time we got home, the Mets were trailing 6–1 and two new patrolmen were parked on the sofa. Norma was up and about and had showered, put on fresh clothes, and combed her hair. Sort of. She was helping Merilee set the kitchen table. It was another kitchen table dinner. Merilee had the salad ready and immediately went to work liberating Lulu's quarter section of the spinach-and-mushroom pie and putting it on the counter to cool.

"Someone," she observed tartly, "has smoked his after-dinner Chesterfield before dinner."

"It's been a stressful day," I acknowledged.

"I would swear we're talking about *two* someones," Norma said, burying her nose in Very's sweater. "Two extremely beery-smelling someones."

"Like Hoagy said, it's been a stressful day," Very said defensively. "For your information, I came very close to losing someone whom I care about a lot."

"But you didn't," Norma said, hugging him tightly. "I'm right here. And I'm not going anywhere."

"Better not," he said, hugging her back.

I looked over at Merilee, whose eyes were shining at me.

Lulu, meanwhile, was starting to whimper impatiently for her pizza.

Actually, Lulu wasn't the only one who was hungry. After Merilee had set some of Lulu's section of pie beside her dinner bowl, we heaped our plates with slices, helped ourselves to salad, sat, and dived in, making yummy noises. Merilee and Norma had wine. Very and I stayed with our Bass.

Norma had barely finished one slice of spinach-and-mushroom pizza before she confessed that she felt an overwhelming desire to climb back into bed.

"Then you should," Merilee said to her gently. "You've had a highly emotional day."

"But I should help you with the dishes."

"Pshaw. Get into bed. And don't forget to brush your teeth."

Norma looked at Very and said, "Will you be up late?"

"Don't think so. I'm super tired myself. I'll join you as soon as I finish stuffing my face. This sausage-and-peppers pie is incredible. I can't believe it—I must have driven by Sal's a million times and never noticed it. He's on my

A-list now." He squeezed Norma's hand. "I'll join you in a little while."

He polished off two more slices before he yawned hugely and said he was going to take a shower and join Norma.

"You do that," I said to him.

"And tomorrow we'll hit the ground running," he vowed. "Cool?"

"Cool."

I bagged up the leftover slices, not that there were many, and stowed them in the fridge while Merilee put the dishes in the dishwasher. The luxury of having a dishwasher in a New York City apartment is not one to be understated.

After that, Lulu and I rode the elevator downstairs for her bedtime walk. The Mets had managed to eke out one more run in the bottom of the ninth off the weakest arm in the Phillies' bullpen. The final score was 6–2. As Lulu and I walked, I mulled over which one of Norma's former authors would have wanted her dead the most. To my mind, Professor McCord was the slam dunk favorite. His high-profile academic, publishing, and TV careers had all crashed and burned, and he was definitely the type to look for someone other than himself to blame. Plus, I thought he was a dickhead. That's why I'd never make an ace homicide detective like Very. I'm guided by my emotions.

I'm also not too keen on the idea of getting shot at.

When we returned from our walk, Merilee was tucked into bed wearing an old Brooks Brothers red flannel nightshirt of mine and reading *Cat on a Hot Tin Roof* by Mr. Tennessee Williams. Lulu climbed eagerly onto the bed next to her, rolled onto on her back, and convinced Merilee to give her a belly rub. I took a long, hot shower, trying—and failing—to loosen up my lower back. Then I climbed into bed, too.

"Penelope Estes Poole thinks we'll be sorry if we don't."

"If we don't what, darling?"

"Have kids."

She turned and gazed at me with an innocent expression on her lovely face. "Well, you certainly have a casual way of springing a life-altering discussion on a girl."

"Just thought I'd mention it."

"The subject has now come up twice this evening. Are you hinting that you want to have kids?"

"Who, me? Hell no. Can't stand the little crumb crushers."

"That's what I thought. So why did you bring it up again?"

"Because she said we'd be sorry."

"By *we* you mean *me*. I've still got time. The tick-tick-ticking of my biological clock isn't something I think about day and night. Right now, for example, I'm thinking about this play that I'm trying to read because you want me to do it." She tilted her head at me. "You're in an awfully strange mood. Even for you."

"It's been an awfully strange day. Even for me. And my wheels are still spinning. Plus I've got a tight deadline. Maybe I'll go over some more of Norma's edits in my office for a while."

"You do that, darling."

She went back to reading Tennessee Williams as I got out of bed, put on my Turnbull & Asser target-dot dressing gown, and moseyed quietly down the hall to my office.

Lulu chose to stay in bed with Merilee. I didn't blame her one bit.

The light under the door of the guest room was out. I turned on my desk lamp and shut the office door softly. Sat down in front of my manuscript, my lower back twinging, and reached for my Rolodex. The Racquet and Tennis Club maintains a confidential after-hours number for members who wish to set up a squash game for the following day. I dialed the number, wondering if the exercise would loosen up my back and save me a trip to the chiropractor.

And wondering about a little something else, too.

CHAPTER EIGHT

Alissa Loeb's death was splashed all over the front pages of the *New York Daily News* and *New York Post* the next morning. The *News* went with a boldface screamer: YOUNG BEAUTY DIES IN SUBWAY STABBING MAYHEM. The *Post,* as per usual, upped the fear factor with SAVAGE SUBWAY STABBER TERRORIZES CITY. The *New York Times* put the story on its front page but parked it below the fold under a one-column-width Sominex headline: PUBLISHING ASSISTANT FATALLY STABBED ON 1 TRAIN. Its story did use the quote about Alissa that Norma gave their reporter on the phone, and, as Very had anticipated, both the *News* and *Post* had lifted the quote verbatim from an early edition, attributing it to "sources said."

Norma looked pale and drawn that morning, and I gathered from the dark circles under her eyes that she hadn't slept well. But she insisted on going to the office just as if it were a normal workday. Wanted to be there for her staff. Very would not allow her to take public transit, so her police security team drove her there.

Before she left she made a special point of telling me that she'd finished reading over the chapter I'd given her and was pleased with my responses to her edits except for a few nitpicks that we could talk about later. I assured her that I intended to go over a lot more of her edits that day, which made her happy. It was exceedingly important for her to keep her mind on work. No secret as to why. If she didn't, she'd keep dwelling on her certainty that it was she, not Alissa, who was supposed to be in that body bag in the morgue.

Merilee had zero desire to look at the newspapers. Instead, she went for a jog around the Central Park Reservoir and was at an Ashtanga yoga class when Very and I headed for the Twenty-Fourth Precinct on West One Hundredth Street in his Crown Vic, Lulu curled up on the seat between us. It was a damp, cold morning. The kind that gets into your bones. I stayed with my trench coat and fedora. Wore my barley tweed suit from Strickland & Sons with a dark blue shirt, pink-and-blue polka-dot bow tie, and my shearling-lined ankle boots.

The Twenty-Fourth was a precinct like any other—hectic, dirty, and loud. People were shouting, phones were ringing. Very led us up a flight of stairs and then past the detectives' squad room to a cluster of interrogation rooms. He deposited Lulu and me in a small room next to one of the interrogation rooms that had a two-way mirror in it. The room had recently been cleaned. The wastebasket and ashtrays were empty. There were no Styrofoam coffee cups on the table. And the floor smelled of Pine-Sol, the same pungent cleanser that the custodian had used on the hallway floors of my elementary school in the little Connecticut town where I grew up. It didn't matter that three decades had gone by. One whiff of Pine-Sol instantly took me back there. Smell is an amazingly strong memory trigger. Vastly underrated in our litany of senses. Someone ought to write a book about it someday. Not me, but somebody.

Lulu climbed up on the table next to me to watch the view in the interrogation room. It was a view worth watching. Richard Groat hadn't oversold Lola Lux, née Jean Donkin. She was a definite babe, with long, shiny black hair parted on one side, slightly uptilted brown eyes set wide apart, arched brows, and a wide mouth with full lips. Her fingers were long and slender. She painted her nails a pale pink. Wore a bit of pale pink lipstick, too. Some mascara on her lashes, not much, and a bit of eyeliner. Lola was long and lean, with broad shoulders. She held herself with dignity and calm as she sat there in her Donna Karan navy-blue pants suit and white silk blouse, considering that two patrolmen had just snatched her up when she was leaving Richard Groat's apartment, driven her to the precinct house, and parked her in an interrogation room. She gave every indication of being someone classy, as opposed to a call girl and the former mistress of a professional hit man. She had a Gucci raincoat folded over the chair next to hers. A Gucci shoulder bag kept it company.

Very walked into the interrogation room, his eyes scanning her file, then looked up at her and smiled. "Good morning . . . Jean. Or do you prefer Lola?"

"Lola, please."

"Lola it is," he said, sitting down across from her.

She raised her chin at him. "And you are?"

"I'm Detective Lieutenant Romaine Very."

"Would you be so kind as to tell me what I'm doing here, Lieutenant Very?" Her voice was low and cool. No trace of a Canadian accent.

"Helping me work a homicide case, I hope."

"A *homicide* case?" Right away, her facial expression became guarded. "Should I be phoning a lawyer?"

"That's entirely up to you. At present you're not being charged with committing a crime or aiding and abetting in a crime. But if you decide you wish legal counsel, that's certainly your right."

She arched a brow at Very, studying him. "Exactly what homicide case would we be talking about?"

"You're not someone who believes in wasting time, are you? Good, neither am I. I happen to live with a woman named Norma Fives. She's the editor in chief of a publishing company called Guilford House. Norma was riding home on the 1 train to the Village yesterday after work with her editorial assistant, Alissa Loeb, when Alissa was stabbed through the heart in the Times Square station by an unknown assailant who managed to get away. It's my job to find him."

Lola moistened her lips with the tip of her tongue, swallowing. "I saw the story on the news this morning. It was . . . horrible. And Miss Fives must be devastated."

"She is," Very acknowledged. "Especially because she'd received two death threats prior to the murder and there's every reason to believe that it was she, not Alissa, who was the intended target."

"How awful. You must be worried yourself, you poor man."

His jaw went to work on a fresh piece of bubble gum. "She's got twenty-four-hour police protection on her, but I'd be lying if I said I'm not worried."

"Given your personal involvement, I'm surprised that they didn't assign a different detective to the case."

"I wouldn't let them. My girl, my case."

Lola reached across the table, put her hand over his, and squeezed it. "I wish a man loved *me* that much." She was a pro, no getting around it.

"Are you sure that one doesn't?"

She frowned at him. "Who would that be?"

"Richard Groat."

Lola sat back in her chair, breathing in and out slowly, before she said, "Okay, now I understand what I'm doing here. I'm involved with Richard, and Norma Fives was his editor before he retired."

"Retired is a tactful way of putting it. The reality is that Norma didn't renew his contract. She dropped him."

"But Richard's not upset about it, if that's where you're going with this, Lieutenant. In fact, he's relieved. He doesn't enjoy writing anymore. Has given it up."

"So I gather. I spoke to him yesterday. In fact, I was with him in his apartment when I got the news of the Times

Square stabbing." He thumbed his stubbly chin. "The two of you seem quite close."

"We are," she acknowledged.

"In fact, he told me that you stopped accepting money from him last year because you felt your relationship had evolved beyond professional. You spend a lot of time at his place. The two of you work out in his home gym. He cooks you dinner. You watch old movies on TV together. You even do your homework there. I understand you're taking an introductory class in American lit at the New School."

"That's right, I am. This week we're reading *On the Road* by Jack Kerouac."

"Good book. Groat's practically your boyfriend, is the impression I get—aside from the part where you still work as a call girl on the nights that you're not with him. Is he aware of that?"

"Of course. We have no secrets from each other. I'm very fond of Richard. He's a dear friend. I just wish his anxiety weren't so crippling. It would be fun to go places with him. But he's unable to leave his apartment."

Very glanced down at her file, tapping it with his index finger. "It says here you were picked up for solicitation while you were employed by the After Hours escort service. Charges were later dropped. Also that you lived with a mobbed-up hit man named Nicholas Dipoto, aka

Slick Nick, and were questioned in connection with his disappearance three years ago. You said that you had no idea where he'd gone or why. He still hasn't turned up, in case you're curious, although if I had to make a wild guess as to his whereabouts, I'd go with the bottom of the East River."

Lola's cheeks colored slightly. "You're not a nice man, are you?"

"I'm not paid to be nice," Very fired back. "You came to New York from Winnipeg to become a fashion model, correct?"

"That was my hope."

"Did you sign with an agency?"

"I did, though it wasn't easy. The first thing I was told was that I was getting a late start. I was twenty-one. They prefer to sign girls when they're eighteen. But Jane Darrow took me on at Clean Cut, which was appropriate, I suppose." She smiled faintly. "We Canadians are famous for being freshly scrubbed and glowing with good health."

"I have a busy day, Lola. Just answer my questions, please."

Her smile disappeared. "I got some catalog work, but that damned camera ages you, I swear. My modeling career was over after two years. To pay my rent I took a job as a hostess at a steak house on Madison Avenue. A couple of the girls there also worked for an escort service. They told me it was strictly aboveboard. That they were nothing more than paid dates for out-of-town businessmen. I gave it a try and was on a 'date' with some guy at an electronics industry banquet at the Warwick Hotel. He had a lot to drink. When the banquet broke up, he assumed I'd be going upstairs to spend the night with him. I hadn't agreed to that. He got very angry, created a scene in the lobby, and the next thing I knew, I was being picked up for solicitation. No charges were filed, but that's how I ended up in your file."

"And how did you meet Slick Nick?"

"At a party one night soon after that. I'd never met anyone like Nicky before. He was exciting to be around. Totally unbound by the rules that most people live by. If he wanted to do something, he just went ahead and did it. He also had a lot of money. He bought me clothes. Took me to Miami, the Virgin Islands, Puerto Rico. Introduced me to a lot of fun people. We had a mad case of the hots for each other. Had sex constantly. After a few weeks, I ended up moving in with him."

"Did you know that he'd served time for assault and battery, larceny, grand theft, and was affiliated with one of the major New York crime families?"

Lola blinked at him. "I didn't, I swear."

"Okay, let's try it this way. Where did you think all his money came from?"

"He told me he was in the restaurant supply business. The way he explained it, a lot of new restaurants go under and those commercial kitchens are worth hundreds of thousands of dollars. Nicky said he'd buy them for pennies on the dollar and then resell them to someone else or salvage them or—or . . ." She trailed off with a weary sigh. "I was still a clueless kid from Winnipeg, okay? All I knew was that he had money and was mad about me and that one day I came home and he'd disappeared. All his clothes were gone. His suitcases, everything. He didn't even leave me a note. I—I couldn't afford to stay there so I cleared out and never saw or heard from him again. I did try calling his friends but they said they didn't know a thing."

"So, what, did you think he ran off with another woman?"

"I didn't know what to think except . . ."

"Except what, Lola?"

"It wasn't the kind of relationship that was built for the long haul. He wasn't the settling-down sort. We never stayed home. I never cooked him a meal. He liked to be on the move. Go to parties in the Hamptons. Fly to resorts. We had sex constantly . . ."

"Yeah, you mentioned that part already."

"Lieutenant, what does any of this have to do with Richard? Why am I here?"

"You're not still sticking with your clueless-kid-from-Winnipeg act, are you? You lived with an organized crime hit man, Lola. Those friends of his that you spoke of? They were also organized crime figures. And you're a professional call girl, which suggests to me there's a good chance you're still in touch with them."

Her jaw muscles clenched. "Meaning what?"

"Meaning if Richard Groat, a troubled author who'd just been axed by his editor in chief, asked you how to arrange a hit on Norma, you'd very likely know who to contact."

Lola glared at him stiffly. "Is this an accusation? Because if it is, then I *am* going to call an attorney."

"Nope. You asked me why your relationship with Slick Nick had anything to do with Richard. I was simply telling you."

"I see. Then kindly allow me to tell *you* something, Lieutenant. First, I totally lost touch with Nicky's friends after he disappeared. I wouldn't even know how to contact any of them. Second, Richard has never, ever mentioned Norma in a negative light. I told you, he's not the least bit bitter about what happened. In fact, he's thrilled to be retired. Money isn't a problem for him. He still earns royalties from his books. I also get the impression that his late wife was quite wealthy. Her suicide nearly destroyed him. The first night I met him, I couldn't believe how messed up he was. I had to be so patient and gentle with him. But he's loosened up so much. He's incredibly smart and funny and sweet. I like him a lot."

"Kind of old for you, isn't he?"

"So what? That's why they have the magic blue pills. Besides, our relationship's not strictly about sex. We enjoy each other's company. We talk and laugh. We're good friends. He may even be my best friend, as crazy as that sounds. I just wish I could get him to leave the apartment, but he won't. He's still deathly afraid to, and still on heavy-duty meds. He'll only leave to see his shrink, whose office is practically next door. And if he gets sick, he has a doctor who makes house calls."

"He has a doctor who makes house calls? That must cost a pretty penny. But he was paying you, what, forty-five hundred a week for your company? I guess he can afford it. Lola, where were you yesterday between five and six P.M.? And don't tell me you were at his apartment—because I was there."

"I wasn't going to tell you that. I was going to tell you the truth. I was with a client. I still have to earn a living, you know."

"Where was this?"

"The Mayflower Hotel on Central Park West."

"What was your client's name?"

"My employer runs a highly discreet service. Her clients rely on her to keep their names private."

"So that's a no?"

She fell silent for a second. "May I be candid with you, Lieutenant?"

"By all means."

"My life hasn't turned out the way that I thought it would when I was growing up in Winnipeg. I didn't marry Mr. Right. Don't have two kids. Don't live in a big house with a two-acre backyard. But that wasn't the life I wanted. I wanted to escape to New York and experience some adventures. And I have. And I hope to continue to experience more adventures before I lose my looks and am forced to settle down."

"You could probably settle down with Richard right now and be set for life."

"You think I'm just interested in his money, don't you? You're totally wrong. He's leaving his entire estate to a medical charity that deals with research into mental health disorders. He made a special point of letting me know that when we first started becoming close. Richard is shrewd and super careful. He's never even let me have my own key to the apartment."

"Meaning he doesn't trust you?"

"Meaning he's super careful, like I just said. But he's still the sweetest, smartest guy I've ever met. I feel lucky to know him. And I swear to you that he didn't ask me to arrange for a hit man to take out Norma." She studied Very from across the table. "I can tell from the look on your face that you don't believe a word I'm saying."

"You're a call girl. In my book, call girls are hustlers."

"You're a cop. In my book, cops are assholes."

Lulu let out a low moan of protest. She doesn't like it when people say mean things to Very. I shushed her. Happily, Lola couldn't hear anything through the soundproof walls.

"Someone tried to kill my girlfriend, Lola," Very said heatedly. "He killed her assistant instead and he's still out there, so I've got no time to go ten rounds with you."

"I'm genuinely sorry about what happened, but I'm not hustling Richard. I told you—we're good friends. Lately, I've been working on him to go for walks in Riverside Park with me. Maybe even get a dog. That would be such a positive step for him."

Very abruptly closed her file. "This is the part of the conversation where I advise you not to leave town."

"I'm not going anywhere. Where would I go?"

"Are you planning to see Richard today?"

"I am. He's making us a veal roast for dinner and we're going to watch an early Hitchcock movie called *The Thirty-Nine Steps* that's a favorite of his. He keeps telling me that if I were a blonde, I'd be a dead ringer for Madeleine Carroll." She stood up, reaching for her raincoat and purse. "Who's Madeleine Carroll?"

"What kind of dog?" Very asked her.

Lola frowned. "Sorry?"

"If you convince Richard to get a dog to take for walks in the park, what kind would you get?"

"A basset hound. I just love basset hounds. They're so adorable with those long ears and . . ." She tilted her head, frowning at him. "Am I imagining things or did you just hear a dog bark?"

◆

"What do you think, dude?" Very asked me after Lola had taken off and we stood there in the little room where he'd parked Lulu and me.

"Are you asking me what sort of impression I got of Lola?"

"Kind of, yeah."

"I think she's someone who has struggled with disappointment ever since she arrived in New York," I said as we left the room and headed past the detectives' squad room. "Her modeling career was short-lived, but she didn't want to slink home and marry an auto-parts salesman, so she stuck around long enough to get mixed up with a mobbed-up dirtbag and become a high-end call girl. I'd also say she's extremely lucky."

"Lucky how?"

"Slick Nick disappeared from her life and she's found a nice, soft landing with Groat, who's incredibly grateful to have her around."

"Yet he doesn't trust her enough to give her a key to the apartment."

"Never forget he was a caper writer," I said as we went down the stairs and started toward the front door. "That makes him savvy and wary. A small part of him no doubt still thinks she's trying to hustle him. My opinion? I don't think she is. She still sees a few clients on the side to maintain her financial independence but I think she genuinely likes the guy. He's gentle and super smart, and he cares about more than just her bod. He's interested in what's between her ears, too, which is why she's making an effort to improve herself by taking that lit class at the New School. Although there *is* something that bothers me about that."

"Which is?"

"I don't remember them teaching *On the Road* in an introductory American lit class."

"That's because you went to college a really, really long time ago."

"Thank you large for that."

"Besides, you went to Harvard. Do you honestly believe a professor can convince a bunch of hipsters at the New School to plow their way through Thomas Wolfe or William Faulkner? Hell, nobody wants to read them anymore."

"Wait, wait. I want to write all this down."

"Bite me."

"Have you spoken to Norma at her office this morning?"

He nodded.

"Did she receive another death threat in the mail?"

"No, she did not."

"What does that tell you?"

"That her would-be killer didn't think it would be necessary to mail her one yesterday—the reason being that he thought she'd be dead today."

"That's a sobering notion."

"I certainly thought so."

We went out the door into what was still a chilly morning, even though it was nearly noon. Lulu started barking as we made our way toward Very's Crown Vic. And kept on barking.

"What's up with her?" Very wondered.

"It's lunchtime and we're two blocks from Scotty's. She wants a tuna melt."

"Are you telling me she can actually smell one of his tuna melts from here?"

"Are you telling me that you doubt she can?"

"I've got a full day. Can't be wasting time there."

"Who says we'll be wasting time? You still haven't met Norma's sister, Amy."

"I know this. So?"

"So she still gives me that tickle in the back of my brain. In my nonprofessional opinion, you need to meet her."

He started his engine with a loud *vrooom*. "Fine. Scotty's it is."

Lulu let out a whoop as Very barreled over to Broadway and double-parked outside of the run-down diner. When we walked in, Amy was serving burgers to a couple in a corner booth.

She lit up when she spotted me and my short-legged partner. "You're back!" she cried out happily.

"Once we sank our teeth into a Scotty's tuna melt again, we couldn't stay away," I confessed.

She stared at Very, who stared right back at her. "So you're *him*, the cop boyfriend. You're like a big-time celebrity. I've seen your picture in the newspaper. You're also a major biscuit. Just between us, you could do a lot better than the Mouse." Amy furrowed her brow. "The folks called me last night. Told me you'd phoned them and said she was sedated but totally okay, except we all know that we never tell our parents anything. Is she? Totally okay, I mean."

"She's fine," Very said.

"You wouldn't be jerking me around, would you? Because I'll beat the crap out of you if you are."

"I wouldn't dare," Very assured her.

Amy looked at me. "He also told them she was staying with one of her authors because he lives in a doorman building with top security. You?"

I nodded.

"That was sweet of you."

"I had nothing to do with it. It was entirely Merilee's idea."

"And this morning Norma went to work today just like any other day," Very said. "She insisted on it."

Amy nodded knowingly. "Wanted to show her staff she doesn't give in to fear. That's the Mouse."

"I really don't like that nickname," he said.

"I really don't care," she shot back. "Sit down and have the best tuna melt in town, cutie. On the house."

"Don't mind if I do," he said as we grabbed a booth.

She gave our tuna melt orders to Scotty, then grabbed the coffeepot and filled both of our cups, eyeballing Very. "Boy, I sure can't picture you two together."

"Why do you hate her?" Very asked, sipping his coffee.

"Hate her?" Amy looked at him in surprise. "I don't hate her. Who gave you that idea?"

"She did."

"We're sisters, okay? Sisters never get along. It's like I told Hoagy—the folks thought she was the golden child and I was a big, dumb lump. But that's ancient history. I like working here and I love my Manny, who usually stops by right about noon to top off his thermos. Yep, here he is—on the dot." Amy smiled at him as he double-parked his cab behind Very's Crown Vic.

Out climbed her wide load of a boyfriend. He lumbered inside, thermos in hand, and kissed Amy on the cheek.

"Come on over and say hi to Hoagy and Lulu again," she said to him. "And this is homicide Detective Lieutenant Romaine Very who, get this, is the Mouse's boyfriend."

Manny greeted me with a wave and grin. Lulu got her ears scrunched. Very was a whole different story. Manny eyed him with a distinct lack of warmth before he said, "Didn't you used to be a narc?"

"Yeah, way back when," Very said. "Why are you asking?"

"Because you busted my kid brother Raoul for dealing, that's why. He wasn't a bad kid. Just wanted to fit in with the other guys in the project, find something to do with himself. I told him, hey, you want to find something to do with yourself, learn how to fix engines. The mechanics at the cab company make good bucks. Or get a hack license like me. But he just wanted to hang out and get high. Fell in with a bad crowd, know what I'm saying? You sent him away for three years."

"Is he out now?"

Manny nodded.

"What's he doing with himself?"

"Exactly what he shouldn't be doing."

"With the same bad crowd?"

Manny gave him a short, unhappy nod.

"Truly sorry to hear that."

Manny stuck his chin out. "You should be. You put him away."

"Manny, be nice," Amy said, swatting him before she went to pick up our tuna melts.

When she returned with them, Lulu promptly disappeared under the table to dive into hers.

"Whoa, this sandwich is damned good," Very said, munching away.

"The best," I said, as I worked on mine.

At my feet, Lulu had nothing to add. She was much too busy.

"I don't write the laws, Manny," Very said, keeping his voice calm. "I enforce them. That's what they pay me for. Raoul wasn't a kid three years ago. He was a man. He showed poor judgment, and he's still showing it now. That's on him, not me."

Manny nodded grudgingly. "You're right. A man's responsible for himself. That's why I've stayed clean. And I've got the sexiest woman in New York City."

"Oh, stop!" Amy swatted at him again, playfully this time, before she went to fill his thermos.

After Manny took it from her, he offered Very a handshake. "No hard feelings, bro?"

"No hard feelings," Very assured him, shaking his hand.

"Sorry to dump my shit on you like that."

"Don't sweat it. Goes with the job."

"And I'm sorry about what happened to the Mouse. I hope you catch the bastard who killed her assistant."

"I'll catch him. Count on it."

Manny let out a laugh. "Damn, he sounds just like Kevin Costner in *The Untouchables*, don't he, baby?"

She said, "Yeah, except Kevin Costner's better looking."

Very grinned at her. "Ow."

"But Costner doesn't have a degree in astrophysics from Columbia," I pointed out.

Amy's eyes widened at Very in amazement. "Do *you*?"

Very nodded.

"Okay, now it all makes sense. You and the Mouse, the two of you . . ."

Very frowned at her. "What about the two of us?"

"You're both nerds."

◆

"You don't suppose Manny and Raoul had anything to do with Alissa's murder, do you?" Very asked me as we sat in his parked cruiser, digesting our lunches. Lulu sat between us mouth breathing the scent of tuna so strongly that we both had to roll down our windows. "That the two of them went after Norma as a revenge thing for me busting Raoul?"

"As a matter of fact, I do suppose it."

Very sat there nodding his head to his own rock 'n' roll beat. "It plays. Except I can't picture either of them sending Norma those death threats in the mail. Hell, where would they even get the idea?"

"From Amy. She could have seen it in an old movie. She could even have been the one who assembled them, mucilage and all."

"You had to work the word *mucilage* into this conversation, didn't you?"

"Admit it, you would have been disappointed if I hadn't. But do you think Amy would actually conspire to bump off her own sister?"

"Sure. Happens all the time. Almost as often as wives bump off their husbands, or vice versa. There are way more family killings than there are random acts of violence. Besides, Amy reeks of resentment to me. She's a fat waitress at a dive on West One Hundred Second whose boyfriend is an even fatter cab driver with a wife and kids back home in Puerto Rico and a loser of a brother who I busted for dealing. Meanwhile, her kid sister is the editor in chief of a prestigious publishing house and *her* boyfriend's a hotshot homicide detective."

"Not to mention a biscuit."

"I was hoping you'd cut me some slack on that."

"You know me better than that, Romeo."

He fell silent for a moment, his jaw going to work on a fresh piece of bubble gum. "I could get a search warrant for Amy's apartment. See if we find any cut-up pages of the *Times Magazine*, the mucilage, and so on."

"But Lulu adores Amy."

"What's that got to do with the price of tea in China?"

"With the *what*?"

"Old expression of my mom's. So what if Lulu does?"

"Her instincts are infallible. She's never failed me. Not once."

"You mean not once *yet,* dude."

"I still find it hard to believe that Amy would be involved."

"And I'd still like to search her place."

"Qualifies as a major shot across the bow, doesn't it? There's no way to walk it back if you make it clear that you consider her a suspect."

"So?"

"So it means she won't even consider coming to the wedding."

"What wedding?"

"You and Norma."

His eyes widened. "Since when are we getting married?"

"It's inevitable."

"But I'm not ready to get married," he protested.

"Don't try to fight it. That'll get you nowhere. Just give in."

He stared out his windshield, jaw working on his bubble gum. "Okay, I'll hold off on the search warrant for now. But I definitely consider her a person of interest, along with Manny—and Raoul, for sure. He's the one who has the axe to grind with me."

"Fair enough. What's your next move?"

"Checking out the security cams at the Mayflower Hotel. I want to find out whether Lola was there at the time of Alissa's killing like she claimed she was. Who's to say she isn't mixed up in this business with one of Slick Nick's old running buddies? Plus her mug shot is in her file. I want to touch base with the plainclothesmen who were on the train with Norma and Alissa and show it to them. Maybe she was right there at the scene of the crime, helping the killer make his getaway."

"I'm not following you. Lola said that Groat told her he was *relieved* when Norma cut him loose, remember?"

"Which may have been a total lie. Could be he was bitter as hell that Guilford House dropped him. Could be he was after some payback. We know he's too housebound to have tried to bump Norma off himself, but he could have masterminded it. Sent her those old-school death threats. Given Lola and an accomplice detailed instructions on what to do. Plotting crimes was how he made his living, right?"

I nodded. "Actually, that all makes an astonishing amount of sense."

"What are you up to?"

"I have a five o'clock drink date with Professor McCord's wife, Jillian Goldenson, at Wan-Q. Until then, my brain belongs to Norma. I'll be parked in my office fully focused on her edits to my manuscript. I'll let you know if I dig up anything from Jillian."

"Good deal. Appreciate your help, dude."

"I'm always happy to oblige." On Lulu's low whoop I added, "We both are."

"Want a ride home?"

"Thanks, but I think my lower back would prefer the cushiony luxury of a taxicab that has a mere two hundred thousand miles on it."

He shook his head at me. "No dis, but you're starting to sound like a middle-aged man."

"Only because I'm starting to feel like one."

CHAPTER NINE

For as long as I'd been an aspiring novelist, successful novelist, and stoned-out wreck of a novelist—which is to say for as long as I'd lived in New York City—there has always been, by unwritten accord, a designated safe haven where literary and theatrical people can meet in public without meeting in public. If a major Broadway star is cheating on her husband with a young slab of muscle, she can safely meet him there for a drink and no one will say a word about it. If a powerhouse agent is trying to lure a major client from another agency, the luring takes place there, sight unseen. Until 1990, the designated safe haven was Trader Vic's in the basement of the Plaza Hotel. Once you'd descended into that famous grotto, you became legally blind. If you saw someone you knew, you didn't see them and they didn't see you. Liz Smith, Cindy Adams, and the other gossip columnists respected this unwritten accord and never so much as mentioned the place.

Sadly, when an attention-starved real estate developer and tabloid clown named Donald Trump bought the Plaza in 1989, he gave Trader Vic's the boot because he thought it was tacky, which set off a cascade of snide jokes followed by a total panic. But, happily, a new safe haven quickly filled the void—Benny Eng's Wan-Q, a retro non-chic Cantonese restaurant two doors down from the rear entrance to the Essex House on West Fifty-Eighth Street.

It was there that I met Jillian Goldenson, the distinguished writer for the *New Yorker* and wife of disgraced historian Alexander McCord. I paused just inside of the door next to the burbling Buddha fountain to remove my trench coat and fedora. Benny, who was a burbling Buddha himself, hung them up for me, patted Lulu on the head, and led us back toward one of the discreet, high-backed wooden booths. My hair was still damp from the shower I'd just taken after my squash game at the Racquet and Tennis Club. Happily, my stiff, achy back—which had not benefited from the hours I'd spent hunched at my desk poring over Norma's astute edits—had loosened up considerably, even though my game was a bit rusty. It had been a good long while since I'd been to the old R and T. It truly was a relic of my great-grandfather's era, but there are times when the connections to my past, particularly the social ones, can come in handy.

And it was entirely possible that this had been one of them.

Wan-Q was discreetly lit, which is to say dim. It kept your eyes off the circa 1957 tiki bar decor. Its extensive menu of "tropicocktails" offered such exotic favorites as zombies and mai tais, which hardly anyone ever drank. Its menu featured bygone finger food favorites such as egg rolls and fried wontons topped in a sticky red sweet-and-sour sauce. But no one ever went to Wan-Q to eat, with the possible exception of my short-legged partner.

Jillian was drinking a double Jack Daniels with one ice cube. I know this because she polished it off as I arrived and ordered another while I sat down and ordered a Kirin beer for myself and some fried shrimp for Lulu, who circled three times under the table before she curled up on my feet. It had been thirteen years since Jillian had spent two days and nights writing a profile of me for the *New Yorker* after I became the first major new literary voice of the 1980s. It gave me no pleasure to observe that time had not been on her side. Journalists who cover wars in far-flung places, not to mention America's own drawn-out, brutal presidential campaigns, age faster than the rest of us do. Jillian was a gritty, hard-boiled reporter who worked hard and lived hard, and it showed. It also didn't help that she chain-smoked Gauloises, those strong, unfiltered French cigarettes that come in the distinctive blue package. She lit another one as soon as she'd stubbed out the one she'd been smoking. Her sexy mane of flaming-red hair was no longer a mane. She'd cropped it so that it wasn't more than two inches long. Also it was no longer flaming. Too many sprinkles of gray. Her blue eyes were no longer mischievous or playful. Just world-weary. She had furrows of frown lines in her forehead, squint lines around her eyes, and a downward turn to her mouth that suggested she seldom smiled. Although she did offer me a faint one when she stuck her hand across the table. I shook it, recalling that she chewed her fingernails to the quick. She wore no makeup or lipstick and paid little or no attention to her wardrobe. Wore a baggy dark brown sweater and rumpled gray flannel slacks.

"I was surprised to hear from you," she said in a voice that had been coarsened by all those Gauloises.

"Pleasantly, I hope."

"Of course," she assured me, giving Lulu a friendly pat on the head. "Can I tell you a secret, Hoagy?"

"You most certainly can."

"You hold a special place in my memory bank. Whenever I look at myself in the mirror and see what a wrinkled, middle-aged hag I've become, I can always look back and say to myself, 'You once fucked the brains out of Stewart Hoag.' Although I really don't think it's fair."

"What isn't fair?"

"That great-looking young guys hold on to their looks longer than semi-hot young babes do. In fact, you're even better looking now than you were then. Not as boyish. I hear you've gotten back together with Merilee."

"It's true, I have. Finally finished a second novel, too. It only took me twelve years. And you don't look like a middle-aged hag, Jillian."

"You wouldn't say that if you saw me with my clothes off," she said as our waiter brought us our drinks and Lulu her shrimp, which Lulu promptly disappeared under the table to devour. "I was crazy about you, you know. You were so talented, funny, and rebellious."

"I was crazy about you, too. You were smart, sexy, and incredibly cool."

She colored slightly. "I thought something more long-term might happen between us."

"So did I."

"Why didn't it?"

I sampled the beer, found it a bit flat, and sprinkled some salt on it to liven it up. "Because two weeks after that amazingly up-close-and-personal profile you wrote of me, I went to the Blue Mill on Commerce Street for dinner with a pal of mine. He bumped into a young actress he knew named Merilee Nash and introduced us. She stared at me with those mesmerizing green eyes of hers. I stared right back at her. And, just like that, my life changed."

"In unadorned English, I didn't stand a chance."

"I'm afraid not."

She watched me drink my beer, studying me curiously. "I'm hearing rumblings from our literary people that your new novel is spectacular. I'm glad you found your voice again. I know you went through some rough times—cocaine, the breakup with Merilee, those schlock ghostwriting gigs. I can't believe that you don't look like a dissipated wreck, but I'm big enough to bury my bitterness and say congratulations."

"Thank you. But one thing confuses me."

"Just one?"

"Why were you surprised to hear from me? Surely your husband must have told you about our recent close encounter of the unpleasant kind."

Her eyes widened in surprise. "No, he didn't. Why on earth were you in touch with Alexander?"

"I was along for the ride at the request of a friend."

"That friend being . . ."

"Here's the deal, Jillian. Everything that I'm going to say from now on is off the record. Deal?"

"Deal. I never betray a source. Wouldn't be where I am if I did."

"The friend was Romaine Very."

She stubbed out her Gauloises and lit another one. "The NYPD's star homicide detective? How did you two become friends?"

"Our paths have crossed several times over the years. I can't be positive, but I think some form of higher power has been playing a cruel joke on us. Hell, it won't even surprise me if I end up being the best man at his wedding."

"Whom is he marrying?"

"My editor, Norma Fives, although he doesn't seem to realize it yet."

Jillian blinked at me. "The Norma Fives somebody tried to kill on the 1 train during rush hour yesterday?"

I nodded grimly. "And killed her assistant, Alissa Loeb, instead. Wait, how did you know that Norma was the intended target, not Alissa? That hasn't been made public."

"I'm a reporter, remember? I hear things." Jillian's tongue flicked over her lips, her eyes gleaming at me with keen interest. "So why would someone want to kill Norma?"

"This is still off the record, right?"

"Absolutely."

"Norma started receiving death threats in the mail a couple of days ago. She's made some enemies lately. Candidate number one was Boyd Samuels, the sleazeball HWA agent who pulled a highly unethical scam on her. She blew the whistle and got him fired. When Lieutenant Very and I paid a visit to Boyd at his apartment, he swore to us that he hadn't sent Norma any death threat. The guy was a total wreck. In fact, he was in such a state of coke and Wild Turkey–fueled despair that as we were leaving, he took a dive off his tenth-floor balcony."

"Which would effectively eliminate him as a suspect in yesterday's subway killing," Jillian said dryly.

"Correct. So we moved on to a couple of other obvious candidates. Due to a mandated budget haircut from her publisher, Norma has had to lower the boom on two longtime Guilford House favorites, Richard Groat and Penelope Estes Poole. Very and I have spoken to each of them, and they both seem at peace with the decision. Penelope is seventy-two and told us she's been ready to retire her Weaverton Elves for a while. And Richard suffers from such acute anxiety that he can't write a word anymore. Like Penelope, he seemed to harbor no animosity toward Norma at all."

Jillian nodded knowingly. "Which brings us to Alexander."

"Which brings us to Alexander. It was Guilford House's lawyers' decision to drop-kick his Truman bio, not Norma's, but she insisted on being the one to deliver the news to him in a conference call."

"Sounds like she's one tough cookie."

"That she is."

Jillian sipped her bourbon, her mouth tightening. "Alexander's ego has taken a huge hit. He loves to go on tour to promote his work and meet his adoring fans, especially the ones who are attractive young women dying to sleep with him. He's also been dropped from *The MacNeil/Lehrer NewsHour,* which means he won't have a chance to boink any cute, young production assistants."

"It seems he also enjoys boinking cute, young editorial assistants. He was having an affair with Alissa. It's possible he broke it off. It's possible Alissa didn't take it too well and threatened to rat him out to you."

"In which case it's possible that she, not Norma, actually was the intended victim and that the formerly distinguished historian to whom I'm married is a cold-blooded murderer."

"He's what Lieutenant Very calls 'a person of interest.' Sorry to have to tell you."

She caught the waiter's eye and raised her empty glass. He nodded, got her a fresh double Jack with one cube and brought it right over. He looked at me inquiringly but I was still nursing my beer. Lulu, however, was more than ready for another plate of fried shrimp.

Jillian took a sip of her Jack, stubbed out her Gauloises, lit another one, and took a deep drag on it, exhaling through her nostrils. "No need to be sorry, Hoagy. He's been sleeping around for years with the likes of Scarlett Bloom, the graduate assistant who torpedoed his Truman book. The man's an insatiable hound."

"You seem rather placid about the whole thing, if you don't mind my saying so."

"I don't mind a bit. If I'm not jealous or upset, what does that tell you?"

"It tells me that you have affairs of your own."

"Affair, singular. I keep an apartment in DC and spend two weeks a month there, unless I'm off covering our latest military misadventure. For the past three years I've been involved with a *Washington Post* correspondent who's divorced and shall remain nameless. We love each other. In fact, we're a well-known couple around Washington. Not here, because no one here gives a damn about who sleeps with whom in Washington, unless it has something, anything to do with the Clintons."

"Have you thought about divorcing Alexander and marrying the guy?"

"I have. *We* have. I think right now that would be cruel timing, since Alexander's career has taken such a hit, but I'm going to talk to him about it in a few months."

"Would you move to DC full time?"

"Probably." Jillian narrowed her gaze at me shrewdly. "I consider myself pretty quick on the draw. It doesn't usually take me more than one beat to catch on, but you're so far out in crazy town that this has actually taken me two beats. You're wondering whether I'm still so madly in love with Alexander that *I* killed Alissa in a jealous rage. I'll admit that it might make sense in the abstract, but in our case it's totally preposterous. The love went out of our marriage years ago."

"Lieutenant Very and I visited Alexander the day Alissa was murdered. He said you were in DC but were flying back to New York that afternoon."

"Correct. I caught the noon shuttle. Made it to Midtown by about two."

"Where did you go when you got here?"

"Straight to the office of the *New Yorker* on West Forty-Fifth to transcribe my notes for a story on Hillary."

"Why didn't you go home to transcribe them?"

She bristled. "Are you *interrogating* me?"

"Just wondering."

"Because I didn't feel like going home."

"What time did you feel like going home?"

"Five o'clock or so."

"Was Alexander there?"

"No. He'd left me a note saying he had a departmental meeting at four. Those tend to go on for a couple of hours. I'm sure a roomful of historians can vouch for his whereabouts."

"Can anyone vouch for yours?"

"No one. I poured myself a Jack, sat down in my office, and marked up the notes I'd just transcribed." Jillian tilted her head at me curiously. "Hoagy, you don't really think I dressed up in a disguise and stuck a shiv in Alissa, do you? Why would I? Between us, I'm glad that Alexander finally got caught with his professional pants down. He's always been fast and loose when it comes to 'borrowing' his adoring graduate assistants' research. He even acts as if they should be flattered that he steals their work."

"He's, what, fifteen years older than you?"

"Seventeen."

"Why did you marry him?"

"He fooled me, believe it or not. And I don't fool easily. But he's an amazingly accomplished bullshit artist. It took me a while to put the pieces together and realize that he was a womanizing hound and slipshod scholar."

"Why didn't you leave him when you did?"

"Because I wasn't interested in anyone else—plus I was spending more and more of my time overseas in war zones. The state of my marriage seemed rather irrelevant." She raised an eyebrow at me. "So you and Merilee are back together for real?"

"It doesn't get more real."

"Are you planning to have kids?"

I sighed inwardly. "Why does this question keep coming up?"

"It's a natural question to ask. She's pushing forty."

"Actually, she's had a head-on collision with forty. The truth is that the prospect of becoming someone's father gives me the jimjams. She knows that, so she's not pressuring me. She still has time. How about you?"

Jillian shook her head. "Not interested. And my guy in DC already has two kids in college from his first marriage. He doesn't want to start another family." She stubbed out her cigarette, running her fingers through her cropped hair. "It's amazing how important a role timing plays in our lives, isn't it? Think about it. If you hadn't walked into the Blue Mill that night, you wouldn't have met Merilee. The two of us, a pair of hip, talented, oversexed young writers, might have moved in together. And I would never have married Alexander, whom I met a few months later."

"All true," I agreed.

Benny came waddling hurriedly over to us now, clearing his throat uneasily. "Pardon me, Mr. Hoag, but I have a call for you from a Lieutenant Very. He said it's important."

Right away, I felt an uptick in my pulse.

I excused myself and followed Benny up front to the cash register, Lulu trailing close behind me. The phone was off the hook on the glass countertop next to a dispenser of paper-clad toothpicks. "What's up, Lieutenant?" I asked.

"Meet me in the Ramble in Central Park as soon as you can."

"*Where* in the Ramble? It's a huge place."

"You won't have trouble finding me." He let out a sigh of pain. "We've got another one, dude."

I felt all the air go out of my body. "*Who*? It's not Norma, is it?"

He didn't answer me. He'd already hung up.

◆

Very wasn't kidding, not that I for one second thought he had been. I had zero problem finding him as I directed my cab driver up Central Park's East Drive. Just past the Seventy-Second Street Boathouse, a half-dozen blue-and-whites, two unmarked Crown Vics, a coroner's van, two forensics vans, and a herd of TV news vans were crowded along the edge of the drive near a footpath that led into the Ramble, Frederick Law Olmsted's signature creation of thirty-eight acres of dense woods, stone ledges, and twisting, hilly footpaths between Seventy-Third and Seventy-Ninth Streets that magically transported city dwellers deep into the country. It was home to many varied species of trees and a beloved destination for the city's bird-watchers.

After I'd paid the cab driver, Lulu and I made our way toward the crowded footpath, where a length of yellow police tape and two broadly built patrolmen were keeping the TV cameramen out.

"What do *you* want?" one of the patrolmen asked me.

"I'm Stewart Hoag. Lieutenant Very sent for me."

"Yeah, okay," he grunted. "He told me to expect you."

"Where is he?"

"Just keep walking. Can't miss him." He stepped aside to let me duck under the tape. My short-legged partner had no need to duck. "Hey, wait, no dogs are allowed at the crime scene!"

"We're going to pretend we didn't hear that," I said as we started along a twisting footpath. Darkness had fallen. When I'd first moved to the city back in the crime-ridden seventies, the Ramble was considered a mugger's paradise after dark. No one dared go near the place. At various times in its storied history, it had also served as a destination for clandestine gay hookups and illegal drug buys. Lately, it was considered a reasonably safe place to walk. Lulu and I strolled the Ramble quite often while I enjoyed my after-dinner cigarette. I lifted my gaze and looked at our building on Central Park West. The lights were on in our sixteenth-floor windows. I wondered if Merilee was standing there in the living room looking down at all the emergency vehicles and news vans and asking herself what was going on.

After about eighteen twists and turns, we finally arrived at the crime scene, which was illuminated by portable floodlights. A body lay under a tarp. The same balding coroner and his same assistant were standing there talking to Very, who was in hyper-overdrive mode. Head nodding to his rock 'n' roll beat. Jaw working savagely on a piece of bubble gum.

"I got here as fast as I could," I said to him, staring at that tarp with the body underneath with total dread. "Who is it?"

He looked at me grimly before he gestured to the coroner to let me have a look.

It was Penelope Estes Poole, the seventy-two-year-old Park Avenue aristocrat, avid horsewoman and longtime author of the Weaverton Elves mysteries. Penelope lay there on the path much the way Alissa Loeb had on the floor of the 1 train—flat on her stomach, a knee bent, her head turned to one side, eyes open. She was wearing a flannel-lined denim jacket, corduroy trousers, and hiking shoes.

Lulu immediately got busy sniffing the hiking trail, nose to the ground, snuffling and snorting.

"Does Norma know?"

Very nodded. "I called her at the office. This was one toke over the line for her, I'm sorry to say. She got so upset she started weeping and couldn't stop. Kept saying she had to get out of there, had to get out of there. Her security detail brought her to your apartment. Merilee had given her a spare key in case no one was home. But it turned out that Merilee was. She made Norma a cup of cocoa, put her to bed, and called me to let me know. I haven't spent much time with Merilee before. She's a really kind person, isn't she?"

"Yes, she is. I don't suppose there's any chance that this was a random mugging, is there?"

"Zero chance." He showed me Penelope's small leather pocketbook, which he'd bagged and tagged. "Found this right next to her body, stuffed full of credit cards and cash."

"And I'm guessing there were no witnesses."

"You're guessing right."

"How was she killed?"

"Here's where it starts to get even more freaky-deaky—the exact same way as Alissa Loeb."

The coroner took a pen from his pocket and pointed to the left side of Penelope's back in the vicinity of her bra line. "Same kind of entry wound in the same location," he informed me. "Same kind of pointed razor-sharp, double-edged switchblade. Won't surprise me one bit if it's the exact same knife. Forensics will have a look with a microscope." He scratched his balding head. "I can't be absolutely sure until I get her on my table but I'm almost positive she died the exact same way as our subway victim. The knife penetrated between her ribs directly into her heart and severed the lower half of her left ventricle. You see a pool of blood anywhere? I don't. She bled out internally. Would have been unconscious in seconds, dead in less than two minutes."

I gazed down at her, my wheels spinning. "Why would the same killer want to kill Penelope?"

"Good question, dude. You come up with an answer, be sure to let me know. I sent a man over to her building to inform her doorman. He was fond of the old girl and real upset. Said she took a brisk one-hour walk every day at four-thirty in the Ramble, rain or shine. She liked to stay fit and the woods reminded her of being in Little Compton."

"So we're talking about an established pattern here. Her killer must have been observing her and planning this."

"Most def," Very said, jaw working on his bubble gum.

"Who found her body?"

"A bird-watcher, shortly before dusk. Mild-mannered little fellow who managed to flag down a blue-and-white on West Drive. He's pretty shook up. That's him sitting on the bench over there with the binoculars, still collecting himself."

"Did he hear anything? See anything?"

"He says no, but we'll try him again tomorrow morning. Maybe some details will come back to him when he calms down. We'll also have forensics comb the earth for fresh shoe prints in the woods surrounding the path. The whole area is cordoned off for now."

"Does her granddaughter, Gretchen, know what's happened?"

Very grimaced. "Not yet, unfortunately. The doorman said she left at around two o'clock to serve as a docent at the Metropolitan Museum of Art, but still hasn't come home. We tried calling her there right away, but she'd already left for the day. No idea where she is now."

"I wonder if she's at that retro disco bar on Second Avenue she likes to hang at with her girlfriends."

"Good possibility. You don't remember the name of it, do you?"

"Stayin' Alive."

"Right, how could I forget?" he wondered aloud, his head nodding, nodding.

Easily, I observed. He was clearly super freaked. This case was now an even bolder-face front-page nightmare. It had started in the Times Square subway station during rush hour yesterday with the stabbing death of Norma's editorial assistant and now, twenty-four hours later, we were standing in Central Park over what appeared to be the identically stabbed body of Penelope Estes Poole, the billionaire doyenne of Fifth Avenue society, who had been one of Norma's best-known and most beloved authors. The mayor had no doubt gone berserk when he got word of it and hollered at Inspector Feldman, who had no doubt taken it out on Very.

"How are you holding up?" I asked him.

"Not real well," he confessed. "I need your whacked-out brain to help me make sense of this, dude, because I am missing something huge here." We moved away from Penelope's body and let the ME go about his business. "I just don't get how the pieces fit together. Why would the same person who tried to kill Norma yesterday and, because of those nineteenth-century subway brakes, killed Alissa instead, want to kill Penelope? And yet the two killings are clearly connected. Same knife. Same MO. They've *got* to be connected. I just can't figure out how, unless we're totally on the wrong path."

"We're not on the wrong path, Lieutenant."

He peered at me curiously. "Why do you sound so sure about that?"

"Because I am."

"Did you pick up anything from Professor McCord's wife?"

"For starters, Jillian knows he's a cheat but doesn't care. She has a boyfriend of her own in Washington. Lives with the guy when she's there, in fact."

"Doesn't sound like much of a marriage."

"Only because it's not. Jillian is quietly savoring McCord's fall from grace because she's known for years that he steals research from his attractive young graduate assistants."

"How does she know that?"

"She's a reporter. Reporters always know those things. She's been giving serious thought to divorcing him and moving to DC full time—but, out of the goodness of her heart, she has decided to wait for this Truman biography firestorm to blow over. For what it's worth, she made it back to New York on the DC shuttle yesterday in time to stab Alissa on the 1 train during rush hour. But I truly don't see it, Lieutenant. The love is gone. And she definitely didn't stab Penelope, because she was with me at Wan-Q when it happened. Speaking of which, she said that McCord was in a departmental meeting at the university yesterday that started at four o'clock and couldn't have been on that subway. Unless, that is, he didn't show up at the meeting."

"We checked. He was at the meeting. And it went on for more than two hours."

"What about today? Do you know where he's been since, say, four o'clock?"

"Teaching a class, then holding office hours. The schmuck's in the clear."

"Okay, then let's step back for a second and work our way through this." I sat down on a bench. Very joined me. So did Lulu, her scent search having yielded nothing useful. If it had, she would have let me know. We sat there for a moment watching the ME and his assistant tuck the esteemed Penelope Estes Poole into a body bag. "Who else is in the mix?"

"There's Richard Groat," Very said.

"Fair enough. But why would Groat want Penelope dead? She was a longtime colleague who'd just gotten the same axe as he had. I don't buy it," I said, tugging on my ear as I mulled it over. "Unless . . ."

"Unless what, dude?"

"Penelope was, what, ten, twelve years older than he is? An attractive older woman. Is it possible that they'd been longtime lovers as well as colleagues, that his wife found out about it and *that* was the reason why she hung herself? Maybe he's been blaming Penelope—and himself—for her death and decided now was the perfect time to do something about it."

"What about the suicide note that his wife tied around her neck? The one that said how sick she was of watching *Raffles*?"

"He could have written that himself in a decent facsimile of her handwriting and destroyed her real suicide note. Nothing to it."

"True enough. If he plotted out this murder, too, then that means he widened the circle again to include his beloved Lola Lux and her designated hit man." He mulled it over for a moment himself, his head nodding, nodding.

"Feels like a bit of a reach to me, but it plays. We can't rule it out."

"Speaking of Lola, Lieutenant, did she show up on the security cams at the Mayflower Hotel at the time of Alissa's murder?"

"I don't have an answer for you on that. Haven't made it over there yet. Before the shit hit the fan here, I got tied up at the house, running a criminal background check on Norma's sister, Amy."

"She gave you that same tickle in the back of your brain that she gave me, am I right?"

"She did. And so did her honey, Manny Rojas. There's just something *off* about them. I can't figure out what it is, so I worked it for a while. Amy got nailed four years ago for trying to walk out the door of Macy's with a winter coat that she hadn't paid for, but she returned it and they chose not to press charges. Otherwise, she's clean. So is Manny, aside from a couple of minor street scuffles. You can't drive a cab in this city without the occasional scuffle. But his loser of a kid brother, Raoul, the one I put away for dealing, he's digging a real hole for himself. I spoke to a friend of mine on narcotics and they have their eye on him for being into serious cocaine trafficking. It's only a matter of time before they land on him hard."

"But what possible connection would they have with Penelope? Why would they want her dead?" I shook my head. "No, I don't like it. Feels askew."

Very smiled at me faintly. "There's another word I never hear unless I'm working a case with you. You trying to cheer me up?"

"Little bit."

"I agree. They have no connection with Penelope that I can come up with. As in zero. None. Nada. I swear, this whole shit show feels like it's been turned on its ear now. *I* feel like I've been turned on my ear. I could have cobbled together a case that Amy was consumed by bitter resentment over Norma's success. She sent Norma the death threats and enlisted Raoul to shank her on the 1 train while Manny waited topside in his cab as getaway driver. I wouldn't call it a strong case, but it was solid enough that I was going to haul in Manny and Raoul and sweat them—until I got *this* call. Now, where am I?"

"You're in Neil Young country, Lieutenant."

Very frowned at me. "As in . . ."

"As in *Everybody Knows This Is Nowhere.*" I took a deep breath, letting it out slowly. "Although I may have picked up some news you can use just before I met up with Jillian."

He perked up. "Oh, yeah? Do tell."

Before I could open my mouth, a patrolman came charging up to us and said, "Victim's doorman just contacted us, Loo. Her granddaughter's arrived home."

Very stirred uneasily and said, "Okay, thanks." To me he said, "It is now my duty to stroll over there and inform Gretchen Poole in person that her beloved nana has just been murdered. As an act of departmental courtesy, we always deliver horrible news in person, never over the phone. I won't be long. I'll meet you back at your apartment."

"I'd like to come with you." I heard a low woof at my feet. "Which is to say *we'd* like to come with you."

"Trust me, dude, you really don't want to. It's the single most painful part of the job—aside from getting shot, that is."

"I don't care. We're coming with you."

Very shrugged. "Suit yourself, but don't say I didn't warn you."

In order to ditch the press mob that was waiting for his statement back by the Seventy-Second Street Boathouse, Very took a trail that circled west and took us over the Bow Bridge, which I swear has been featured in every romantic comedy ever filmed in New York City. Then we made our way east, past the Bethesda Fountain and toward Fifth Avenue.

"Why do you keep looking over your shoulder?" Very asked me.

"Because I want to make sure no one hears what I'm about to tell you."

"Would this be the something new that you may have for me?"

"It would."

"Is this the real reason why you wanted to come with me?"

"Not totally. Lulu and I happen to specialize in moral support, and you look as if you could use a truckload of it right now."

"So you're like, what, being a friend?"

"Call it whatever you want."

He let out an impatient sigh. "Okay, that'll be enough of the touchy-feely. Tell me what you're not telling me."

"You may recall that I get back spasms whenever I have to ride around in your total wreck of a cruiser."

"How could I forget? You've only complained about it six times since yesterday."

"So today, before I met Jillian at Wan-Q, I loosened it up by getting in a game of squash at the Racquet and Tennis Club with my old chum Zach Talcott. Zach's younger brother, Buzzy, was the one who was engaged to Gretchen Poole until, Gretchen told us, she dumped him because she couldn't imagine spending the rest of her life being married to such a humorless waste of skin, or words to that effect. Zach did me a favor and phoned Buzzy for me and . . . are you listening?"

"I'm listening, I'm listening."

"Got an entirely different version of their breakup."

"Which was what?"

"When you and I paid our call on Penelope, Gretchen flared up at her out of nowhere when she wouldn't let the subject of Buzzy drop. Do you remember that?"

"Um, vaguely. So?"

"So that was no trivial thing. Turns out it was a glimpse of the *real* Gretchen, who isn't the sweetly poised and perfect Smithie she'd like people to think she is. It seems she has a serious anger management problem and is prone to violent and outright abominable behavior. Buzzy gave Zach the names of two other guys who've met up with her dark side."

"Dude, where are you going with this?"

"You may have noticed that Gretchen took a bit of a shine to me when we paid our call on them."

"Gaga is more like it. She's madly in love with you. Once again, so?"

We crossed Fifth Avenue and started toward Penelope's building, which was not yet surrounded by a crush of TV cameramen, photographers, and reporters, but would be as soon as her identity was made public. Two patrol cars were already parked out front, ready to keep the sidewalk clear and maintain order. Or try. One of the patrolmen nodded to Very as we entered the lobby.

Penelope's doorman looked terribly sad. "It was my privilege to serve Mrs. Poole for twenty-seven years, Lieutenant. She was one of a kind. Always a chipper smile on her face and a kind word. She was genuine class. A lady. They don't make them like that anymore."

"I'm sorry for your loss," Very said. "How did Gretchen seem when she got home?"

"A bit on the giddy side. I think she had had a cocktail or two with her girlfriends. I . . . gathered she didn't know yet, and I didn't feel I should be the one to tell her."

"You handled that properly," Very said to him. "It's on me to tell her."

The doorman reached for the house phone. "Shall I?"

"Please."

When she answered, he said, "Lieutenant Very and Mr. Hoag are here, Miss Gretchen . . . Yes, Lulu as well. They wish to come up. It's a matter of some urgency . . . I'm aware that your grandmother hasn't returned from her walk yet. It's you with whom they wish to speak . . . Very well, thank you."

He gestured to the penthouse elevator.

"Yo, I'm still waiting for an answer," Very said as we started toward it. "Where are you going with this?"

"Lieutenant, do you trust me?"

"Yeah, I do. I have no idea why, but I do. Why are you asking?"

Once the elevator doors closed behind us, we shot our way straight up with a *whoosh* to the penthouse.

"Because, with your permission, I'd like to try to move Gretchen around a little."

"Move her around how?"

"By smooth talking her into showing her hand."

His eyes widened at me. "Wait, are you telling me that *Gretchen* is our killer?"

"I'm telling you that we're about to find out."

CHAPTER TEN

The elevator doors opened into the vastness of the living room, which was extremely dark until Gretchen flicked on the chandelier.

She was standing upstairs on the second-floor landing. "Sorry for the creepy lighting," she called down to us. "I just got home and I absolutely *had* to change out of my docent outfit."

The beautiful young Park Avenue heiress descended the curved staircase barefoot, wearing a pale pink cashmere crew-neck sweater that made her creamy, flawless complexion look even more creamy and flawless, and a pair of snug-fitting dark-wash jeans that did her toned, shapely body absolutely no harm. How many times a week had she told us she worked out with a personal trainer? I couldn't recall, but she was getting her money's worth. Not that money was an issue for her. She was carrying a pair of shearling-lined moccasins and neatly folded pale gray cashmere socks.

"Join me in the sitting room, please," she said, padding her way across the living room and turning on some lamps in there. She sat in one of the chintz armchairs, wriggled her toes, and gently massaged her slender feet, sighing with relief. She was twenty-five but had the feet of a pampered child, soft and pink. "Ah . . . that's better." She put on her socks and moccasins and sat back, tossing her silky shoulder-length blond hair. "The Met makes docents wear grown-up leather-soled pumps. I've just spent hours on my feet in them, then walked over to Stayin' Alive and stood at the bar drinking tequila sunrises with my girlfriends, fighting off a foursome of truly twerpy bond traders before I walked home. My poor little feet were killing me."

Once again, as on our previous visit, her huge blue eyes kept straying in my direction and lingering the way a woman's eyes do when she wants you to know she's interested in you. Only this time she made no effort to be subtle about it. The doorman was right. She was definitely a bit tipsy. "Where's Lulu?" she demanded to know. "I want to give her a hug."

"Wandered off somewhere. She likes to explore. She'll turn up."

Gretchen raised her perfectly sculpted chin at Very and said, "Now then, Lieutenant, what's so important that you need to see me even though Nana isn't home yet?"

"Gretchen, I'm extremely sorry to tell you that your grandmother isn't going to be coming home. She was found stabbed to death in the Ramble at twenty minutes past five. We tried to reach you at the Met but you had already left."

Gretchen let out a gasp, her eyes widening in shock. Almost immediately, tears began to spill out of them and run down her cheeks. I got up and offered her my linen handkerchief. She took it, dabbing at her tears, and impulsively grabbed my hand with her free hand, clutching it tightly. I stayed where I was and let her clutch away. "Nana was *murdered*? You can't be serious. This can't be happening. It can't be. It just can't. I can't even . . . What on earth happened to her, Lieutenant?"

"She was taking her walk in the Ramble. According to your doorman—"

"Redfield. His name is Redfield."

"Redfield said she took a brisk one-hour walk there every day at four-thirty."

"Yes, she l-loved the Ramble . . ." More tears streamed down Gretchen's gorgeous young face. She dabbed at them with my handkerchief, still clutching my hand. "It reminded her of Little Compton."

"A bird-watcher found her face down on the path. According to our coroner, she was stabbed through the heart in a manner remarkably similar to Alissa Loeb's murder on the subway yesterday. Exact same sort of knife wound. We've found no trace of the knife, no witnesses."

"Was she . . . violated?"

"The coroner found no evidence of that."

Gretchen let out a sigh of relief. "Oh, thank God."

"Nor was she mugged. Her pocketbook was right next to her body, filled with cash and credit cards. Our forensics people have to dust it for prints. Someone will drop it by later."

Gretchen suddenly became aware that she'd never let go of my hand. "Oh, I'm so sorry. Please forgive me," she said, releasing it.

"Not to worry," I assured her, returning to the sofa.

Gretchen sat there in stunned disbelief. "I just . . . I don't understand. Why on earth would anyone want to kill *Nana*?"

"I'm afraid I don't have an answer for you yet," Very said. "And I wish I could tell you what, if any, connection there is between her murder and Alissa's. But I can't. Honestly? This may be the strangest case I've ever encountered. I don't understand it myself. Not yet anyhow. But I'll figure it out. You have my word."

Gretchen sat there in grief-stricken silence for a moment. "It's just dawning on me that there are people I have to notify. Nana's sister, Alma, in Little Compton. She can let the rest of the family know. And I suppose I should call Nana's lawyer. He handled all her financial affairs a-and . . . I'm sorry, I'm finding this is all kind of overwhelming."

"It absolutely is," Very said gently. "You've suffered a terrible loss. Tell me, is your phone number here unlisted?"

"Yes, it is. Why?"

"Because that means the press won't be calling you every thirty seconds, which is a good thing. But if I were you, I wouldn't leave this apartment for a few days. There'll be TV cameramen and newspaper photographers camped out downstairs in droves for a photo op of you. I'll station some men there to try to contain the frenzy. If I can help in any other way, please let me know." Very removed his card from his wallet and set it on the coffee table.

She sat there gazing at it. "Thank you, Lieutenant. You're very considerate."

I said, "Gretchen, you really shouldn't be alone at a time like this. Do you have a relative or close friend who can stay here with you?"

She let out a mournful sigh. "I do. I'll call my cousin Beth. She lives two blocks away and won't mind staying here with me for a few days. We get along well, and she's an actual grown-up in her forties—an investment banker, levelheaded. She'll know how to handle this much better than I will."

"That sounds like a good plan," Very said. "We'll leave you to it. And you have my deepest sympathies." He got up off the sofa.

I stayed put. I wasn't going anywhere yet. I was waiting to hear from my partner, who was still busy exploring the giant two-story penthouse. "Gretchen, I just have one quick question before we go, if you don't mind."

She gazed at me with those gorgeous eyes of hers. "Of course, Stewart. You can ask me anything. What is it?"

"Why did you do it?"

"Do what?"

"Kill your grandmother. Is it because she found out?"

Gretchen gaped at me in shock. "I'm sorry, I'm still in a bit of a daze and the words coming out of your mouth aren't making sense to me. Because she found out *what*?"

"That it was you who killed Alissa on the 1 train yesterday. Not that you intended to. You really meant to kill

Norma—and would have if there hadn't been that troublesome issue with the brakes. We'll get to that in a second. But, first, why did you kill your nana?"

"I still don't understand what you're talking about, Stewart," she said, her voice becoming distinctly chillier. "But I must tell you that what you're saying is in really bad taste and I'm deeply offended. What is wrong with you? Are you out of your mind?"

"No, but you are. I played squash this afternoon at the R and T with Zach Talcott. We still play together from time to time. You were engaged to Zach's younger brother, Buzzy, for a while, remember?"

Gretchen's mouth tightened. "As if I could forget. And I *don't* wish to discuss Buzzy right now."

"Well, that's too bad, because we're going to. Zach phoned him for me from the locker room so I could get his version of why the two of you broke up. According to Buzzy, violent tantrums are a featured part of the package with you. He said that you once got so furious with him because he wanted to see a different movie than you that you raked his face with your nails and drew blood. He still has the scars to prove it. The exact words that Buzzy used to describe you were *batshit crazy*. He told me that *you* didn't break off the engagement. *He* did."

"Well, he would say that, wouldn't he?" Gretchen fired back. "That lazy do-nothing would never admit the truth. Honestly, Stewart. You mustn't believe a word of that."

"Buzzy also gave me the names of two other guys with whom you've been romantically involved and had, shall we say, painful breakups. One was a high-end furniture designer named Steven Ames, whom you punched in the nose because he showed up twenty minutes late for a small dinner party you were throwing. Punched him hard enough that you broke it and he had to have corrective surgery."

"Steven's a total wimp," she said dismissively. "Not to mention a bed wetter."

"The other was a rising associate at a white-shoe law firm named Mike Williams."

"A sicko pervert." Gretchen's cheeks mottled angrily now. "After we'd been sleeping together for a couple of weeks, he confided to me that he wished to, and this is an exact quote, 'fuck me in my pooper.' I'm Gretchen Poole, not an alley cat in heat. He also told me that he was desperate to suck on my toes, as if I'd put my precious toes in his filthy, disgusting mouth."

"What did you do to *him*?" asked Very, who'd grown keenly interested.

"I didn't so much as lay a finger on Mike, if that's what you're wondering."

"What *did* you do to him?" Very demanded, raising his voice.

She heaved a sigh. "You're beginning to annoy me, Lieutenant."

"Likewise," he shot back.

"Just answer the question, Gretchen," I said in a soothing voice. "Please."

"Okay, fine. But only because you asked me nicely, Stewart. I picked up the phone and got Mike disbarred for grossly immoral conduct and sexual deviancy. He's now a commercial real estate broker in Palm Springs, California." She gazed at me invitingly. "Mind you, I'd let *you* suck on my toes for as long as you wanted to, Stewart."

"Thank you, I'm flattered. I think."

"Would you like me to take off my slippers and socks so that you can stare at them some more?"

"That's an awfully tempting offer, but not right now."

"Are you sure?"

"Quite sure."

"Well, if you change your mind, just let me know, because I must tell you what a thrill it would be for me. You're my idol, you know. The ideal man. Gifted, gentlemanly, and *so* handsome." She let out a sigh of regret. "I've tried incredibly hard to keep my hopes up, but the men in my life so far have been such a source of disappointment to me."

I tugged at my ear. "I'm sorry to hear that, but you still haven't answered my question. Why did you kill your nana? Oh, and I have another question. Did you use the same knife on her that you used on Alissa?"

Gretchen frowned. "Why would you ask me that?"

"Because the lieutenant's forensics people have microscopes that are so powerful they'll be able to prove if it was the same blade. And then you'll be totally cooked."

Very narrowed his gaze at her. "Gretchen, if there's any truth to what Hoagy's alleging, it's my duty to advise you to call your attorney before you say another word."

"You surprise me, Lieutenant," she said to him calmly. "Given your stellar arrest record, I wouldn't expect you to be so naïve. Nana was an Estes Poole, as am I. With her gone, I'm now the wealthiest woman in New York. I *own* this city and every public official in its employ. You can't lay a finger on me. No one can. So if Stewart wants to know why I killed Nana, I have no problem telling him." Gretchen paused, pursing her soft, delectable young lips. "The sad truth, which Nana did a courageous job of hiding from the public, is that she suffered from dementia. That was why she needed my help with the last two Weaverton

Elves novels. And that was why she was perfectly content to retire the series when Norma delivered the bad news. Her memory was slipping. She could no longer keep the plot details straight. She also became easily confused. So, in the months and years to come, how could I be certain that she would keep the promise she'd made to me? 'You're my granddaughter,' she told me. 'I love you, and I swear to you I'll never tell a soul.' Yet she had a strong, healthy body. Would probably have lived another ten, possibly fifteen years. Meanwhile, her dementia would have advanced to a point where I could never be sure that she wouldn't tell someone about it."

"Wait, wait," Very interjected. "Time out on the field. Wouldn't tell someone about *what*?"

Gretchen let out a sigh of regret. "I made one huge mistake. It never occurred to me that she would go searching for anything in my bedroom closet. She never, ever went into my bedroom suite. Why would she? It's *mine*. Yet there she was, poking around on the top shelf."

"What was she searching for?" Very asked.

"Some old family photos, or she claimed. I told her they weren't in my closet. Why on earth would *I* have them? She had no coherent answer for me. Just looked at me in confusion, which was a symptom of her dementia."

"What *did* she find in your closet, Gretchen?"

"I think I have a pretty good idea," I said. "But why don't you tell us, Gretchen? It'll mean more coming from you."

"Of course, Stewart. Among other things, a tote bag containing the *New York Times Magazine*, a pair of scissors, sheets of copier paper, letter-sized envelopes, and a bottle of mucilage."

"Damn, somehow I knew I'd hear that word again." Very scowled at Gretchen. "So it was *you* who sent the death threats to Norma. Why in the hell did you do that?"

"Because I wanted to scare the crap out of her, that's why. So that when I talked Nana into changing her mind and demanding that Norma offer us a contract for two more Weaverton Elves novels, she'd cave and agree to keep the series alive. Norma simply couldn't kill off the Elves. They're an institution. They mean so, so much to millions of readers."

"You mean they meant so, so much to *you*," I said.

Gretchen colored slightly. "It's true, Stewart, they do. Norbert, Filbert, Noel, Virgil, Chester, Hans, Cuddles . . . they've been my family since I was a girl. I never had anyone else. No brothers or sisters. No parents. Just Nana and the Elves. I love them, and helping her with these last two books has been like a dream come true for me. In fact, I actually rewrote quite a bit of the last one. And I told Nana I'd be happy to take over all the writing for her if she'd let me. It's the only thing that's given my life any sense of genuine purpose. Ever since I graduated from Smith, I've been drifting from one volunteer job to another, looking for a purpose. The Elves are my purpose. And Norma Fives was going to take them away from me. I suppose that there are a lot of highbrow intellectuals who think the Elves are silly. They're *not* silly. They believe in truth and goodness, and they deplore evil. I started reading the series when I was ten. I've read all thirty books at least six times, and I—I simply refused to believe that there would be no more of them. I begged Nana to call Norma and *insist* that Norma reconsider. She was Penelope Estes Poole, for heaven's sake. If Norma continued to say no, she could simply have gone over her head. All it would have taken was one phone call to the publisher. But Nana agreed with Norma that it was time to retire them. Her mind was made up, and I couldn't budge her. She could be an incredibly stubborn old bitch sometimes."

"You felt tremendously thwarted, I gather."

"I did, Stewart," Gretchen acknowledged.

"Just out of curiosity, why did you mail Norma the death threats from Grand Central Terminal?"

"Because I was spending a lot of time there doing my research and planning. I also didn't want them to originate from this zip code."

Very said, "You scared Norma, good and plenty, I'll give you that. But you didn't accomplish a thing, did you?"

"No," she said angrily. "I was so damned frustrated."

"And I take it you don't handle frustration well."

"If only Nana had seen things my way, none of this would have happened."

"But why did you kill Norma? Or try to kill her, I should say."

"Because I'm Gretchen Poole, that's why," she said indignantly. "Understand this, Lieutenant. If you take something important from me, then I'm going to take something important from you—such as your life. It could not be simpler."

I glanced over at Very, who was staring at her in disbelief. He'd told me he'd encountered some strange cases before, but Gretchen Poole qualified as a whole new level of strange.

"Unfortunately," she continued, "that decrepit old subway train lurched to a stop, I got hurled forward, and the knife went into Alissa's back instead of Norma's. Which I feel terrible about. I liked Alissa. It was bad luck for her. And for me, too, because I didn't accomplish my goal. And I'd planned everything so carefully, too."

"Is that right?" Very was still staring at her in disbelief. "How so?"

"I believe I told you gentlemen that I love to haunt consignment clothing shops for disco-era treasures. Well, let me tell you, I stumbled upon a rare find a few months ago—a Bloomingdale's reversible men's suede-and-nylon jacket from the seventies. Suede hates to be rained on, as I'm sure you know, Stewart."

I nodded. "It gets all spotted."

"Exactly. So some genius came up with the idea of lining it to become a nylon rain jacket. Two jackets in one. Such a clever idea, don't you think? Yet it was a total flop. Bloomingdale's couldn't give them away. The jacket was too roomy for me, but I loved it so much I added it to my collection of oddities, never realizing that one day it would serve such a vital function. I wore an oversized hooded sweatshirt from a sporting goods store underneath it to give me a stocky appearance, a cashmere crew-neck sweater of my own under that, and a pair of men's vintage baggy, flared blue jeans. Underneath them, I wore a pair of my own dark-wash hip-huggers. A stocking cap and big wraparound sunglasses completed the disguise."

"What about those work boots and work gloves that you had on?" Very asked.

"They were my own from when I volunteered at Habitat for Humanity. I didn't think anyone would find the work boots strange if I wore them with my sweater and jeans once I'd stripped off my disguise. If anything, they'd figure it was a new style and go out and buy themselves a pair. When it comes to fashion, I happen to be something of an influencer." Gretchen brightened. "Do you like that word, Stewart? I think I just made it up." Briefly, she seemed to have amused herself before she turned serious again. "I studied myself in the mirror that morning very carefully and was positive that no one would be able to tell whether I was a man or a woman."

"And you don't wear any jewelry," I said. "Don't even have your ears pierced, not that anyone would have been able to see your ears under that hooded sweatshirt and stocking cap. I'm curious, why is that?"

"Because I don't need to wear jewelry. I look perfect just the way I am. And because people expect me to wear it."

"So it's a form of rebellion?"

"I don't know if I'd put it that way. I just don't like to do what's expected of me."

"Yeah, kind of catching on to that," Very said.

"I had the knife tucked inside the sleeve of my sweatshirt and carried a ziplock bag in my jacket pocket with a dish towel in it. Also a cheap Nike nylon gym bag that folded up pocket-sized."

"Gretchen, would you mind telling us about the knife?" I asked.

"Not at all, Stewart. I used a pointed razor-sharp, double-edged switchblade, four inches long. And, believe me, I went to a lot of trouble to get it. I had to take the subway to a really scuzzy sporting-goods store way out in Queens. Rego Park, no less. I dressed like a sloppy college student, messed up my hair. I passed for someone totally ordinary, which is never easy for me. It takes a lot of effort." She glanced at me, coloring slightly. "Did I just sound terribly conceited?"

"Little bit."

"I'm sorry. I can't help myself sometimes."

"Don't worry about it. There's nothing wrong with having a healthy sense of self-esteem."

Her blue eyes sparkled at me in delight. "It's *so* incredible that you understand me, Stewart. I've never met another man who does. You make me tingle all over. You do know that, don't you?"

"I know that you were telling us about the scuzzy sporting-goods store way out in Rego Park."

"Yes, I was. The owner, who had the world's worst body odor, gave me all kinds of attitude. Smirked at me, treated me disrespectfully. 'Why do you want a knife like that, girlie?' he wanted to know. I said I was entering a graduate program in social work at Columbia University and that I wanted it for personal protection because I'd be living in a really dangerous neighborhood. He said, 'If I was you, I'd pack a gun.' And I said, 'Yes, but you're not me, are you?' Grudgingly, he showed me how to press the button to flick it open. And he warned me to be damned careful with it or I'd hurt myself. I paid him in cash, and after I rode the subway home, I went up in my room and practiced using it for over an hour until it felt practically like an extension of my hand." She paused, breathing slowly in and out. "And then I was ready to take Norma's life."

"Would you mind walking us through how it went down?" I asked.

"Not at all. I arrived at Guilford House's office building on West Fifty-Second Street in full disguise shortly before five o'clock and waited on the sidewalk for Norma and Alissa to leave work for the day. When they did, I followed them to the subway entrance on Broadway and West Fiftieth Street, waited on the platform with them for the downtown 1 train, and got on the same car with them."

"Were you aware that two plainclothesmen were tailing them, too?"

"Of course, but they were such obvious lummoxes that all I had to do was follow them as well." She glanced at Very. "Honestly, Lieutenant, your superiors should recruit a higher grade of talent. I intend to send the mayor a memo on the subject." Then she turned back to me. "Times Square was the first stop on the line. I had decided in advance that I'd stab Norma there because it's an incredibly busy station with a million stairways and passageways. I'd made several visits there, combing the passageways until I'd found a perfect place where I could disappear for the ten seconds that I'd need to make my wardrobe change after I knifed Norma and sprinted out the door of the train, across the platform, and up the stairs. It required me to make a hard right and dart my way through the rush hour crowd toward the Grand Central shuttle. Just before the shuttle platform there are those stalls where they sell newspapers, candy, popcorn, and things. I'd found an L-shaped corridor there that led to a locked door marked CUSTODIAL SERVICES—STAFF ONLY. A supply closet, I imagined. Mops, buckets, and so on. No one who didn't work in the station would have any reason to go into that corridor. I'd tested it twice during the evening rush hour for a full five minutes. Not a single custodian used the supply closet either time. And all I needed was ten seconds to make my wardrobe change. I'd timed it in my bedroom with a stopwatch."

"Sounds as if you had a precise, thorough plan," Very said.

"Of course, I did. I don't do anything halfway. That's how mistakes happen."

"Except a mistake did happen," he pointed out. "You killed Alissa, not Norma."

"That wasn't me," she fired back hotly. "That was the train operator."

"The knife was in your hand, not his."

She said nothing to that. Just glared at him.

I said, "Alissa was your friend. Do you still feel badly about what happened to her?"

"I do, Stewart," she said, her voice softening. "And thank you for asking. I'm terribly sad about it. But I truly didn't have a chance to think about it at the time. I was too busy elbowing my way out that subway door, dashing across the platform and up those stairs to that little hallway outside of the custodial closet. I pulled the ziplock bag from my jacket pocket, sealed the knife in it, and put it in the Nike bag. Then I removed my work gloves, took off my baggy flared jeans, hooded sweatshirt, stocking cap, and shades, and stuffed everything in the Nike bag. Then

I reversed my rain jacket and walked—didn't run—to the nearest exit carrying the Nike bag and wearing my loose-fitting suede jacket, cashmere sweater, and slim-cut jeans. I took a flight of stairs that came out in Times Square and strolled my way uptown, watching the police cars streak by with their sirens blaring. Worked my way up Broadway, then over to Seventh Avenue, and when I got to Fifty-Eighth Street, I ducked in the rear entrance of the Essex House."

I smiled at her. "Let me guess, you used their lady's room to tidy up."

"Why, yes. As a matter of fact I did."

"Sure, the Essex House is *the* best pit stop in town. The rear entrance means you don't have to go through the lobby. I use their men's room all the time. The men's room at the St. Regis is excellent, too. It's in the basement down the hall from the barber shop. Where is the lady's room at the St. Regis? I've never—"

"Dude, you're babbling," Very interjected.

"Sorry, but Midtown's choicest pit stops are one of my favorite subjects. Somebody should write a book about them. Not me, but somebody. I apologize, Gretchen. I didn't mean to stray off topic."

She gazed at me warmly. "It's quite all right, Stewart. I could listen to you talk for hours and hours. We're soul-mates, you know."

"That's kind of you to say. You ducked into the Essex House and . . ."

"And when I went into the lady's room, I ran my fingers though my hair and made sure I looked presentable. I found no traces of blood on my face and checked to make sure that the sleeves of my sweater were okay, which they were. I did find a spot of blood on my right work boot, which I wiped off with a wet paper towel. I wasn't able to do a perfect job, but it just looked like a smudge. I didn't dare wash the blood off the knife in there. Someone could come in and find me. I waited until I got home, locked my bathroom door and washed it in the sink with soap and water, then scrubbed the sink with Ajax."

"Why didn't you just ditch the knife in a trash can?" Very asked her.

"Because I'd gone to so much trouble to get it. It was *mine*. You can understand that, can't you?"

"I suppose," Very said.

"After I'd stowed it and my subway costume in the Nike bag, I put it on the top shelf of my closet with the tote bag that was filled with the makings of those death threats."

"Which reminds me," Very said. "Norma didn't get one this morning. You didn't mail her one yesterday because you expected her to be dead today."

"That's correct."

"Kind of whack if you stop and think about it," he reflected, thumbing his stubbly chin. "Not that this whole thing isn't whack."

"Gretchen, you've been just a tiny bit coy with us, haven't you?"

She blinked at me. "Have I? How so?"

"Earlier, you mentioned that when your grandmother was searching through your closet that 'among other things' she found the tote bag with the makings of the death-threat letters. By *among other things,* you meant she found the Nike bag, too, didn't you?"

Gretchen lowered her eyes, swallowing. "She did, not more than an hour after I'd stowed it there. She wondered what I was doing with such a cheesy nylon sporting-goods bag when I have so many nice leather designer bags. And she was so assertive and headstrong that before I could move a muscle, she'd yanked it off the shelf, unzipped it wide-open, and found my knife and subway slayer costume. 'What is all this, Gretchen?' she demanded to know. I never, ever lied to her. She was too good and kind a person to lie to. Besides, I'm not someone who ever lies. I'm Gretchen Poole. I have no need to lie. Did that . . . sound terribly conceited, too, Stewart?"

"No, that was fine."

"Good, I'm glad you feel that way," she said, smiling at me warmly. "So I told her exactly what I had done. She was genuinely sorry that I was so upset about the Elves that I'd resorted to such 'extreme behavior,' as she put it, but it still didn't change her feelings about retiring the series. That was Nana. Once her mind was made up it was final. But she did promise me that she would never, ever tell a soul about what I'd done. It would be *our* secret and it would go to the grave with her. I believed her, too, because she loved me. We hugged and kissed and cried a little. And then, as far as she was concerned, the matter was closed. Never to be mentioned again."

"But something happened, didn't it?"

"Well, yes, Stewart," she admitted. "As I was lying in bed last night, I started worrying about her dementia. What would her condition be like in five years? Or ten? Could I absolutely count on her mind staying lucid enough for her to keep her promise to me? Or was it possible that the truth could just come tumbling out one day while she was talking to someone, especially because she liked her sherry. I wasn't comfortable with the situation. I found it highly unsettling. So unsettling that I couldn't sleep. Just lay there, squirming under the covers. I always sleep in the nude. You're too much of a gentleman to ask, but I know you were wondering so I thought I may as well tell you.

I just love the feeling of silk sheets against my smooth, bare flesh. But not last night. As I lay there, squirming, my wheels were spinning and I started coming around to the idea that I needed to be proactive. I did have all the gear right there in my closet, and it so happened that I had an ideal scheduling opportunity today. So I decided to dispose of Nana as an act of self-preservation. I took the Nike bag with me when I went to the Met, which, as you know, backs up onto Central Park on Fifth Avenue only a few blocks uptown from the Ramble. I finished my shift at the Met at four o'clock, walked down to the Ramble, ducked into a heavily wooded area where not a soul could see me, and changed into my costume. Then I waited for Nana to enter the park for her four-thirty constitutional. She liked to walk by the sailboat lake when she entered the park. She strode briskly, as you might well imagine, her head high, shoulders back. I followed her from a careful distance until we got deep into the twists and turns of the Ramble."

"It's very private in there, isn't it?" I said.

"Yes. Too private for some people, who worry about getting mugged. Not Nana. She never gave in to fear of any kind. I watched and listened and when I was sure no one was coming, I rushed up behind her, opened the switchblade in my right sleeve, covered her mouth with my gloved left hand, and used all my strength—and I'm stronger than I look—to stab her in the left side of her back where I'd stabbed Alissa, which had proven to be very effective because it went between her ribs and directly into her heart. She let out a moan of pain and fell to the ground, face-first, as soon as I released her."

"Did she see that it was you who had stabbed her?"

Gretchen shook her head. "She never saw me. Why do you ask, Stewart?"

"I was just wondering if she had a chance to look you in the eye before she died."

She frowned. "I find that a strange thing to wonder about."

"I find it strange that you find it strange. But, please, continue."

"I pulled out the knife and fled into the deep woods off the path. Bagged the knife. Tore off my costume same as I had in the Times Square station. The only difference was I was wearing my Met docent outfit under it. A blouse, sweater, slacks, and pumps. I'd made plans to meet a couple of girlfriends at Stayin' Alive sometime between five and five-thirty. I hid the Nike bag behind a rock near the entrance to the park and strolled over to the bar. I arrived first and checked myself over in the lady's room. I looked fine. Not a hair out of place. My pumps were a bit muddy but a damp paper towel took care of that. By then my girlfriends had arrived, and, let me tell you, I have never needed a tequila sunrise quite so much as I did at that moment. I practically chugalugged it. We chattered and giggled and I had a second one, though I drank that one much more slowly. Still, I was in high spirits by the time I made it back to the park, retrieved the Nike bag, and came home. In fact, I only got here a few minutes before Redfield phoned from the lobby to say you were here."

It was now, at long last, that I heard Lulu begin barking. She was far away. I'm talking eerily far away, like in that episode of *The Twilight Zone* when the little girl disappears into another dimension and her parents can hear her but not see her.

"LULUUU!" I called out.

Lulu continued to bark. I got up and followed the sound. We all did. She was somewhere upstairs, so up the stairs we went.

"LULUUU!"

I followed the direction of her barking down what seemed to be a half mile of hallway until it got louder and louder and—at long last—I arrived at the open doorway to a luxurious bedroom suite, where I could hear her clearly but still couldn't see her.

Damn, it really was like that *Twilight Zone* episode.

"Is this your bedroom?" I asked Gretchen, who had a tense look on her face.

"Yes," she answered softly.

"LULUUUU!"

She let out a whimper from somewhere. I'll admit it, I was starting to get the willies. Okay, I just lied. I'd had the willies ever since the elevator doors had opened and Gretchen greeted us from the top of the stairs.

It was an enormous suite, lavishly furnished. A French provincial four-poster bed with a huge antique trunk at the foot of it. A wardrobe cupboard, desk, tall dressers with drawers—all of them antique French provincial. The carpet was a plush, creamy white. There was a seating area with a chintz loveseat and armchair. Gretchen's reading nook. On the top shelf of her built-in bookcase was her hardcover collection of all thirty of the Weaverton Elves books in numerical order. Penelope had always numbered them at the bottom of their spines.

There were two doors, both closed, that I imagined led to her closet and bathroom.

"LULUUUU . . ."

Again, she let out a whimper. But this time I got down flat on the floor and found her.

She was under the bed.

She let out a low whoop when she saw me. She'd discovered something important under there that she was nudging at with her large, bulbous black nose.

"What have you got, girl?" I reached for it and pulled it out.

It was the Nike gym bag.

"Good girl!" I said as she crawled her way out. I rubbed her tummy until she made happy argle-bargle noises. "What a good girl!"

"As I mentioned, I'd just gotten home when you arrived," Gretchen said. "Didn't have a chance to finish tidying up. I was still barefoot, remember?"

"How could I forget?" I said.

"Are you telling us that the bloody knife is still in there?" Very demanded. "The one that you used to murder your grandmother?"

"Yes, I'm afraid so."

"No need for you to be afraid, I'm sorry to say," Very grumbled unhappily. "I didn't obtain a warrant from a judge to search this penthouse. That means the contents of the bag will be inadmissible in court."

Gretchen gazed at him with a look that I can describe only as total pity. "You're such an intelligent man, Lieutenant, yet I still don't think you understand the reality of the situation that you find yourself in. I'm Gretchen

Poole. I will never, ever be charged with committing these murders. I will never even be brought to trial. At most, I'll have to spend a stint in a sanitarium somewhere. While I'm there, I'm going to try to write an Elves book entirely on my own. I look forward to the challenge. I need a challenge. I think that's what has been missing from my life, to be honest."

"That and sanity," Very said.

She frowned at him disapprovingly. "You don't understand me at all, do you?"

"I understand that you're rich, privileged, and nuttier than my Aunt Stella's fruitcake. I understand that you're going to take a nice little ride to the Nineteenth Precinct with me now. I'm not going to cuff you, Miss Poole, because your knife is tucked safely away in the Nike bag and because you've got nothing to fear, or so you claim." He put on a latex glove before he picked up the Nike bag. "So come along. We're going to the house."

"I'm still wearing my slippers. May I least put on a pair of shoes?"

"Where are they?"

"In the closet," she said, indicating the door behind her.

He opened it, his mouth agape. "My God, you must have a hundred pairs in here. Who wears this many shoes?"

"I do. My Arche slip-ons, please. The olive-green ones."

"Which ones are . . ."

"Here, I'll get them," I said. Merilee was a major Arche fan and owned a pair very much like the ones Gretchen described. I found them and set them on the floor next to her feet so that she could step out of her shearling slippers and into them. She rested her hand on my shoulder to balance herself, caressing it ever so slightly.

"Thank you, Stewart. And a jacket for later, please? My belted Armani?"

As I helped her on with the soft leather jacket, she let out a soft purr of pleasure. "You are such a gentleman. I wonder if Merilee has any idea how lucky she is."

"Actually, I'm the lucky one."

"That's certainly not the way I see it. Oh, and I'm going to need a scarf, please. May I just . . ." She reached into the closet for a cranberry-colored silk scarf that was hanging from a group of hooks with several other scarves, then whirled and came away with a switchblade that she flicked open and pointed at both of us, her eyes suddenly ablaze.

"I've got to give you your props, Gretchen," Very said, staring at the pointed razor-sharp, double-sided four-inch blade. "I've run into my share of crazy women, but you've just officially made the top of the list."

"I'm not crazy, Lieutenant. Just practical. I figured as long as I'd trekked all the way out to Rego Park, I may as well buy two knives in case I ever needed another one. And, as it turns out, I did. Now, I want the two of you . . ." On Lulu's low moan of protest, she quickly said, "*Three* of you to leave right now. This is a private residence and you have no business here."

"Yeah, we do." Very whipped out his SIG and pointed it at the center of Gretchen's chest. "I'm taking you in. I'm not a twenty-three-year-old editorial assistant. I'm not a seventy-two-year-old Park Avenue dowager. I'm a trained police officer and I have a job to do." He held out his left hand, palm up. "Close that switchblade, put it in my hand, or so help me God I'll shoot you dead right where you stand. Do it *now*!"

Gretchen was immediately terrified. And docile. And she did exactly what she was told. Meekly closed the knife. Reached over to put it in his hand . . .

And then at the very last second flicked it open and stabbed him deep in the meat of his open hand. Before the blood could even begin to spurt, she'd slashed his gun hand with savage speed, the SIG falling to the carpet and Very letting out a groan of pain. I grabbed Gretchen by both wrists, grappling with her as Lulu growled ferociously and sank her teeth into her left calf, which sent Gretchen into such a fit of rage that she managed to yank her knife hand free and slash me across the cheek. I felt a searing pain and then blood started pouring down my face. By now Very had retrieved his SIG from the floor with his bloody hand and fired a shot into the wall six inches to the left of Gretchen's head.

"The next one goes right between your eyes," he promised her, grimacing in pain as the blood poured from his hands.

"You still don't get it, do you?" she said to him coldly. "If you murder me, you'll end up in prison for the rest of your life."

"It'll be worth it," he said as he struggled to maintain his grip on the gun with his gashed, blood-slickened fingers.

Gretchen saw her chance and took it. In the blink of an eye, she darted into the bathroom and slammed the door behind her, locking it.

As Very let out a string of curses, I went stumbling out of the room with blood streaming down my neck and found a bathroom across the hall. I held a hand towel against my face and neck. Not only was my cheek on fire but my jaw seemed clenched in place. I could hardly move it at all. I gathered up every towel I could find and returned to Gretchen's room, then fell to my knees and swaddled Very's hands in them.

"Thanks," he gasped. "You okay?"

"Uh-uh. Can't . . . t-talk."

"Really? There might be an upside to this after all."

"Vewy funny." The towel I was holding to my face was already so saturated that it was beginning to drip blood. I tossed it aside—fuck Gretchen's creamy white rug—and applied a fresh one. Then I shrugged out of the blood-soaked jacket of my barley tweed suit from Strickland & Sons and took a towel to it, hoping my genius of a dry cleaner would be able to rescue it. My shirt and tie were history.

"Not to worry," Very said to me as he sat there wincing in pain. "We'll get stitched up at Lennox Hill ASAP. Think you can you bring me that phone from her nightstand?"

I brought it to him. He rattled off a number for me to dial that wasn't 411. I dialed it and held it next to the side of his head for him as he phoned it in, speaking in crisp shorthand. Then he told me I could have the phone back and we both sat there on the rug with our blood-soaked towels, Lulu circling around us, whimpering helplessly.

"GRETCHEN?" Very hollered through the bathroom door. "There'll be a dozen cops here in five minutes. You may as well come out of there. If you don't, I swear I'll pump an entire magazine through that door!"

"You'd just be wasting your time, Lieutenant," she responded through the locked door in a calm voice. "This is a huge, L-shaped bathroom. You'll never hit me. Besides, I'm too pretty."

"You're a crazy bitch is what you are."

"There's no cause to be crude. It must be the product of your upbringing."

"I had an excellent upbringing. Much better than yours. And I'm not crude. I'm pissed off. My leg was just getting back to normal and now I've got knife wounds on both hands."

"I didn't get a scratch on me," Gretchen boasted. "I never do. Would you believe I don't have a single scar anywhere on my body? I've never had surgery, not even my tonsils. I've never broken a bone. Never had a serious gash. I'm flawless."

"You remember to keep telling yourself that from the comfort of your padded cell," Very said. "And, correct me if I'm wrong, but didn't Lulu just sink her teeth into your leg?"

"She's a gentle lamb. Didn't break the skin. She was just trying to scare me. Besides, these jeans are rugged, American-made denim, not that flimsy crap from China. A small manufacturer in South Carolina makes them for me. I'll give you the name of the company, Stewart. You need to own a pair."

By now we could hear the sirens heading our way.

Very sat there staring down at the blood-soaked towels around his hands. "Damn, we've been through some weird cases together, but this one? This one's turned out to be totally whack."

"Vewy."

"Yeah, dude?"

"It's vewy whack."

"You got that right."

The penthouse elevator had arrived in the living room downstairs. I could hear heavy footsteps on the marble floor way off in the distance. Husky voices called out for Very. He hollered in response, but they couldn't hear him. Seeing as how he was the one guarding the bathroom door, gun in bloodied hand, I got up, went down the long hallway to the staircase, and showed them where to find him.

◆

Merilee, Lulu, and Norma were waiting for us when they discharged us from the emergency room, where we'd shared neighboring beds just like brothers-in-arms. Unlikely brothers, but brothers nonetheless. The slashes on Very's gun hand were superficial and had just required disinfecting and bandaging. But the stab wound in the meat of his left palm was a deep puncture. They numbed it with four shots of novocaine, stitched it, bandaged it, shot him full of antibiotics, and gave him some pain pills for when the novocaine wore off. They wanted to see him again in the morning to change the dressing and examine the wound for swelling. When it comes to emergency room medical treatment, cops get the best of care.

As for me, after they'd disinfected the two-inch diagonal slash across my right cheek, I got two shots of novocaine of my own—which hurt like hell, by the way—and then they stitched up the wound. The doctor explained that I was having trouble unclenching my jaw, and therefore speaking normally, because I'd suffered some damage to the muscles and ligaments that attached to my temporomandibular joint. But the damage would most likely heal on its own. No surgery required. He gave me an antibiotic shot and some pain pills, placed me on a diet of liquids and soft foods, and scribbled down a set of jaw exercises for me to do when I felt up to it. He wanted to see me again in a week.

"On the plus side," he said to me, "you're going to end up with a dueling scar that'll make you the envy of all your friends."

"It's true, you're going to get an awesome new author photo out of this, dude," Very said as we headed out to the waiting room. When I didn't respond, he said, "Whoa, this is like a dream come true for me. I get to talk as much as I want and you can barely open your mouth."

"Vewy?"

"Yeah, dude?"

"Fuck woo."

Norma, who had been through a hell of a lot of trauma over the past three days, ran to him and hugged him tight, tears streaming down her face. "I was *so* worried about you. If anything ever happens to you, I'll *die*."

"Nothing's going to happen to me," Very assured her. "Hell, I've only been wounded twice in my whole career."

"Both times since you met me," she pointed out, sniffling. "I'm bad news for you. You should dump me."

"Not going to happen, Baby Girl. Besides, this is nothing more than a deep cut. I could have done worse with power tools in my basement workshop."

"You don't have a basement workshop. Or any power tools."

Merilee, who'd become a bit more accustomed to having the man in her life end up in the emergency room, still looked plenty upset herself and hugged me tight before she released me and inspected my bandaged cheek with a critical eye. "I always wondered what it would be like to live with a pirate. Just do me a favor and please skip the whole peg leg scenario, okay?"

When I didn't come back with a quick, witty retort, Very said, "He has trouble talking."

She raised her eyebrows. "Stewart Stafford Hoag has trouble talking? Call the *Times*."

"Vewy funny," I said with some difficulty as Lulu began whimpering, moaning, and trying to climb up my leg. When I bent over to pet her, I felt a sensation of pressure in my face, which I imagined would translate to excruciating pain once the novocaine wore off. I stroked her to assure her I was perfectly okay. "You wah vewy bwave, Wuwu."

Merilee's green eyes danced at me with amusement. "Is it my imagination or do you sound exactly like Elmer Fudd?" She dabbed at my mouth with a tissue. "Except I don't remember Elmer drooling. Or should that be dwooling? Oh, this is going to be *so* much fun."

"Ha ha." I responded with what now had to suffice as a witty comeback.

"Can we please get the hell out of here?" Very demanded.

"By all means," Merilee said.

As we started for the hospital's entrance, Norma tugged at my sleeve. "Hoagy? I don't mean to be a pest but I still need that edited manuscript back from you pronto. Will you be clearheaded enough to work on it?"

I nodded, which was much easier than trying to talk.

And out the automatic opening doors the five of us went into the New York night.

CHAPTER ELEVEN

I'm sorry to disillusion you but Gretchen Poole did, in fact, get away with murder.

Make that two murders, not to mention the criminal assault of an NYPD homicide detective and of the first major new literary voice of the 1980s. She was a Poole, let us not forget. She owned the city, and with that ownership comes the sort of power that most of us can barely imagine.

She never came to trial. Was never even publicly charged with the savage stabbings of Alissa Loeb and her own esteemed grandmother, Penelope Estes Poole. Instead, her lawyer huddled in private with the Manhattan DA in a judge's chambers and brokered a deal to commit her for a period of three years to a sanitarium in Westchester County that was not, just to be clear about this, officially designated as a facility for the criminally insane. It was a cushy hideaway for members of the privileged class who suffered from substance abuse as well as behavioral issues, such as rage. While there, Gretchen would undergo intensive psychiatric sessions to address her anger management problem. She would be reevaluated after eighteen months and, if it was determined that she was calm and stable, be placed under house arrest in her penthouse on Fifth Avenue wearing an ankle monitor for the remainder of her sentence.

The NYPD officially classified her nana's murder in the Central Park Ramble as a random act of violence. The fact that Penelope was stabbed the same exact way as Alissa Loeb had been stabbed twenty-four hours earlier—with what forensics determined to be the same exact knife—was never made public. No connection between the two killings was ever made public. The fact that Alissa had been an editorial assistant at the same house that had been publishing Penelope Estes Poole's Weaverton Elves books for the past thirty years did not merit so much as a mention in the press. New York City was the publishing capital of America, after all. Such minor coincidences do happen.

There was no drumbeat in the tabloids that a switchblade serial killer was on the loose, terrorizing New Yorkers, because there were no more switchblade killings. No arrests were ever made and the story faded quietly away, just like the mayor wanted it to. Scarcely another word was written about it.

I know what you're thinking—things like this aren't supposed to happen in real life. But they do. Usually, you simply don't hear about them. You're hearing about this one.

Detective Lieutenant Romaine Very, whose beloved Norma had been targeted by Gretchen and came within inches of being murdered, was furious with the way it went down, as was Very's superior, Inspector Dante Feldman. In fact, Feldman had to be talked out of resigning from the NYPD by the mayor—whose campaign, you will be surprised to learn, had been financed in large part by Penelope Estes Poole, as had that of the Manhattan district attorney. I was plenty pissed off myself that Alissa's parents never saw their daughter's killer brought to justice. But in my non-chosen second career as a ghostwriter of celebrity memoirs, I've dealt with the rich and powerful numerous times and have learned, repeatedly, that the rules the rest of us live by don't apply to them. So I took whatever small morsels of satisfaction I could get out of

Gretchen's sentence. For starters, it meant she wouldn't be able to dress up in her vintage disco clothes and drink tequila sunrises with her friends at Stayin' Alive for three whole years, by which time the retro-chic club would no doubt have faded into pop-culture oblivion. It also meant that she was about to find out how much more difficult it would be to write a Weaverton Elves novel from scratch than to tweak one of her grandmother's existing manuscripts. Brutally difficult, in fact. I won't go so far as to suggest that it would drive her nuts, because that ship had already sailed, but she might find it humbling. Assuming that Gretchen was capable of being humbled.

I was sworn to secrecy about what had really gone down. The only person in the world I told was Merilee, because I never keep the truth from her. She was disheartened, of course, but far from shocked. After spending fifteen years in the movie business, she was incapable of being shocked by anything that had to do with the dark depths of human behavior.

The only person Very told was Norma. He couldn't keep such a secret from her, he told me. Unlike Merilee, Norma was utterly livid that Gretchen wouldn't be spending the rest of her life in a maximum-security prison growing pasty and fat and possibly getting knifed in the shower. Norma wanted to call a press conference and scream her head off. She still harbored the illusion that life was supposed to be fair. But, with huge reluctance, she came to accept that Gretchen's lightweight three-year sentence was already a done deal and promised Very she would keep the truth to herself. She was also grateful to him for trusting her with the truth. She took it as a measure of his love for her.

I spent the days after Gretchen had gone Zorro on my cheek seated at my desk, drinking espresso through a straw and poring over Norma's highly perceptive edits. I was glad to have my book to work on. It took my mind off the nightmare that Gretchen had put us through. Merilee made me a vat of hearty bean-and-vegetable soup which she then pureed so that I could slurp it with a spoon. She was also a wizard with organic corn hominy grits and soft-boiled eggs. The pain in my jaw wasn't intense enough during the day for me to resort to taking any of the pain pills the doctor had prescribed, which was a good thing because those damned things make my brain foggy. But I did take one at night, because lying down made my jaw throb. It took me a week, working from dawn to dusk, to finish going over Norma's edits. A Guilford House messenger came to our apartment and picked up the manuscript for her.

That same day I returned to Lennox Hill to see the doctor who'd stitched me up. Once he removed the stitches, my jaw muscles began to respond to the exercises he'd given me, which consisted chiefly of slowly opening my mouth as wide as I could, holding it open for a count of thirty, and then slowly closing it. I was supposed to do this several times a day. I was quite diligent. However, I still talked like Elmer Fudd.

"Your normal speech pattern should return as the ligaments and muscles heal," the doctor promised me. "If you find that they don't, we can send you to a speech therapist."

"No, please don't," Merilee said to him teasingly. "I like him this way."

Two days after my stitches came out, a memorial service was held for Boyd Samuels, former vice president of Literary Synergy for the Harmon Wright Agency, at the Frank E. Campbell funeral chapel on Madison Avenue and East Eighty-First Street. I had never liked the guy but I showed up for it. For some reason I felt I owed it to him. His parents, a perfectly ordinary-looking fifty-something couple from Cherry Hills, New Jersey, were there. No one from HWA bothered to show up except for my agent, Alberta Pryce, aka the Silver Fox, who was the head of the literary department and also the only person in the entire agency who had a shred of human decency. The two of us sat together in the vacant chapel.

Afterward, we went down the street to the bar at the Carlyle Hotel and downed a couple of aged Balvenie single-malt scotches as she kept staring at the fresh dueling scar on my cheek.

"I don't wish to be indiscreet, dear boy, but you know what really happened, don't you." It was a statement, not a question.

I nodded.

"But you can't tell me, can you." Again it was a statement, not a question.

I shook my head.

"I won't try to wheedle it out of you. I'm just happy for you that you're alive and will be here to see your novel published after all these years. Which reminds me, we should start working the Algonquin this week."

So Lulu and I began meeting her for drinks every day at five thirty at her table in the lobby of the fabled Algonquin Hotel, where the likes of Dorothy Parker, Robert Benchley, and Alexander Woollcott had once held court. While Lulu sat at my feet and devoured small plates of pickled herring, I accepted congratulations from the array of important editors and critics who made a special point of stopping by our table. Each and every one of them wanted to know what I'd done to my cheek.

To each and every one, Alberta responded, "I encouraged him to take up fencing. Stupidest thing I've ever done in my life—other than passing on *Jaws* when Peter Benchley asked me to represent him."

After Norma had reviewed my comments on her edits, she phoned and briskly informed me that she had a few nitpicks she wished to go over with me. She wondered if I'd mind stopping by the office. I suggested we meet for lunch instead. She said she never did lunch. I told her she'd do this lunch or she wouldn't get the first look at my next novel.

She let out a gasp. "You have an idea for another novel? Okay, I'm in. Where do you want to meet?"

It was a measure of just how driven Norma Fives was that she agreed to meet me for a tuna melt at Scotty's, knowing full well she'd encounter Amy there. But she didn't know she'd also run into Very, Merilee, and Lulu. I'd decided we needed another small celebration of sorts.

Very, Merilee, and I sat in a corner booth and drank coffee while we waited for Norma to arrive. The cuts on Very's gun hand were healing nicely, but he was still wearing a thick bandage on his stab wound, which he allowed still hurt like hell.

Lulu, who is not known for her patience when it comes to food, was already under the table at my feet, devouring her tuna melt, when Norma walked in.

Amy spotted her right away. At first the look on Amy's face was chilly, but then she melted, rushed over from behind the counter, and gave her scrawny kid sister a bear hug. "Hey, Mouse."

"Hey, Amy," she said, her voice muffled by Amy's meaty shoulder.

I don't know if it was all the emotional horror of the past weeks or the simple, uncomplicated fact that Norma hadn't seen her big sister in years, but she broke out into tears. They both did, standing there hugging each other.

After they'd had their good cry, Amy led her over to our table.

Norma stopped abruptly, looking at Very and Merilee in confusion.

"I thought we were meeting here to work," she said to me.

"And you will," said Merilee, who was still enjoying her role as my celebrity spokesperson. "But first you have to join us for a tuna melt. I must apologize for Lulu's manners. She's already gotten a head start. Amy? Four of Scotty's finest, please."

"You bet, hon. Coffee, Mouse?"

"I guess."

Norma sat down next to Very, visibly ill at ease. She was like a cat who'd just been let out of her carrier in a strange apartment. Very put his arm around her and gave her a smooch on the forehead. She sipped her coffee and soaked up the diner's atmosphere, which was warmed by Merilee's glowing smile. Slowly, she began to relax. And, after Amy had brought us our tuna melts and she'd taken her first bite, she was sold.

"You know what, Romeo? I like this place," she said. "In fact, I think we should hold our wedding reception here."

He blinked at her. "I'm sorry, did you just propose to me?"

"I most certainly did."

He chewed thoughtfully for a moment, mulling it over.

She stared at him. "You could say something, you know. It doesn't have to be a soliloquy. Although something along the lines of, 'Cool, Baby Girl, I want to marry you, too,' would be nice."

He nodded. "Sure, why not."

"*That* was real romantic," she said to him.

He furrowed his brow. "I'm just . . . taken aback, is all. I figured I'd be the one who'd propose to you."

"You figured wrong, Romeo. I beat ya."

"So what's the deal?" I asked. "Are you two getting married or what?"

"Guess we are, dude."

"Congratulations. Hey, Amy! They're getting married! And the reception's going to be here!"

"Woo-hoo!" she cried out.

There was widespread applause, hoots, hollers, and whistles from everyone else who was packed into Scotty's diner—all six of them.

Although Merilee, I noticed, seemed a bit crestfallen.

"What's wrong, blond person?" I asked.

"This is terribly petty of me, darling, but I miss your old voice. I know I shouldn't, because it means your jaw has healed and you feel better, but I was getting rather fond of living with a cartoon character."

"Aw, I can bwing it back any time, you wascally wabbit. It's vewy easy."

"Thank you for that, darling." To Very and Norma she said, "And congratulations to the two of you. I've spent enough time around you now to know that you're going to make each other incredibly happy."

"Hey, what about the two of you, dude?" Very demanded.

"What about us, Lieutenant?"

"You're not married. You *were* married, but you're not married now."

"And we're going to keep it that way," Merilee said firmly. "If it ain't broke, don't fix it. I learned those words of wisdom a long time ago from Mike Nichols."

I said, "Really? I learned them a long time ago myself—from Maynard G. Krebs."

Norma frowned at me. "Maynard G. *who*?"

"Don't make me feel old, Norma, or I'll have to hurt you."

"And he's a dueling master now, don't forget," Merilee pointed out.

I gazed at her, smiling. "You know what, Miss Nash? I'm awfully fond of you."

"I'm right there with you . . . Mr. Fudd."